Frank Sewall

The Pillow of Stones

Divine Allegories in their Spiritual Meaning

Frank Sewall

The Pillow of Stones
Divine Allegories in their Spiritual Meaning

ISBN/EAN: 9783337042172

Printed in Europe, USA, Canada, Australia, Japan

Cover: Foto ©Andreas Hilbeck / pixelio.de

More available books at **www.hansebooks.com**

THE

PILLOW OF STONES.

DIVINE ALLEGORIES IN THEIR SPIRITUAL MEANING.

BY THE

REV. FRANK SEWALL.

"Which things are an allegory."—GAL. iv. 24.

PHILADELPHIA:

J. B. LIPPINCOTT & CO.

LONDON: 16 SOUTHAMPTON ST., COVENT GARDEN.

1876.

BY THE SAME AUTHOR.

THE HEM OF HIS GARMENT.

SPIRITUAL LESSONS FROM THE LIFE OF OUR LORD.

TO

CHARLES HENRY AND MARY ALLEN

Affectionately Dedicated.

3

CONTENTS.

PAGE

I.—THE PILLOW OF STONES; OR, HOW TO OBTAIN A TRUST IN THE DIVINE PROVIDENCE . 7

II.—THE TEMPTATION OF EVE; OR, THE BEGUILEMENTS OF THE SENSUAL MAN 23

III.—NOAH'S DOVE; OR, THE SOUL SET FREE . . 45

IV.—MELCHIZEDEK'S OBLATION; OR, THE SACRAMENT OF THE SUPPER OF THE LORD 64

V.—ABRAHAM AND SARAH IN THE LAND OF ABIMELECH; OR, THE DIVINE ADAPTATIONS OF TRUTH TO MEN 82

VI.—HAGAR'S RETURN TO HER MISTRESS; OR, THE SUBMISSION OF THE RATIONAL 107

VII.—ISHMAEL RESTORED TO LIFE; OR, THE SPIRITUAL REASON 125

VIII.—THE ETERNAL LAMP; OR, HOW FAITH IS TO BE PRESERVED 144

IX.—THE ALTAR OF INCENSE; OR, THE FACULTY OF WORSHIPING GOD 160

1*   5

6　　　　　　*CONTENTS.*

PAGE

X.—THE SHEPHERD-BOY MADE KING; OR, THE LORD'S
CHOICE *versus* MAN'S CHOICE 176

XI.—THE ARMOR-BEARER MADE HARP-PLAYER; OR, THE
DIVINE TRUTH PROTECTING AGAINST EVIL SPIRITS 194

XII.—THE MONEY IN THE SACK; OR, HOW THE TRUTH
MAKES FREE 210

THE PILLOW OF STONES.

I.

𝔗𝔥𝔢 𝔓𝔦𝔩𝔩𝔬𝔴 𝔬𝔣 𝔖𝔱𝔬𝔫𝔢𝔰; 𝔬𝔯, 𝔥𝔬𝔴 𝔱𝔬 𝔒𝔟𝔱𝔞𝔦𝔫 𝔞 𝔗𝔯𝔲𝔰𝔱 𝔦𝔫 𝔱𝔥𝔢 𝔇𝔦𝔳𝔦𝔫𝔢 𝔓𝔯𝔬𝔳𝔦𝔡𝔢𝔫𝔠𝔢.

And he took of the stones of that place, and put them for his pillows, and lay down in that place to sleep.—Gen. xxviii. 11.

OUR Lord, when He was on earth as the Son of Man, "had not a place where to lay his head." Jacob of old, when he journeyed away from his father's house, lay his head, when night came, upon a pillow of stones. In the divine words of Scripture, "Jacob went out from Beer-sheba, and went toward Haran. And he lighted upon a certain place, and tarried there all night, because the sun was set; and he took of the stones of that place, and

(7)

put them for his pillows, and lay down in that place to sleep. And he dreamed, and behold a ladder set upon the earth, and the top of it reached to heaven: and behold the angels of God ascending and descending on it. And, behold, the Lord stood above it, and said, I am the Lord God of Abraham thy father, and the God of Isaac: the land whereon thou liest, to thee will I give it, and to thy seed."

Jacob was a man like ourselves, journeying on his earthly road. What occurred to him was a token that we are all here in some way connected with heaven and with the angels and with the Lord. The Lord was watching over Jacob, and, as he slept upon his hard bed, the angels were seen by him ascending and descending above him. What is here related of Jacob as a visible and external event, is truly taking place with all men, more or less, not in a visible and external way, but in a hidden spiritual way, in the course of their journeying from a natural to a heavenly state of

life. Since God's Word is true, and since it
tells us of the spiritual life, the life of the soul,
it must be that in some hidden, unconscious,
spiritual way, we who live and toil, who believe
and doubt, who pray and trust, who are now
anxious and fearful, and now at peace and
filled with thankfulness and rest,—that we, in
this day, are making our journey from a place,
a state of life, in which we have been, to one
before us yet unknown.   There comes for us a
"going down of the sun," the time of night
and the time of rest.   We, too, must find our
pillow; and if it be such a pillow for us spiritually as was Jacob's naturally, we shall see
the ladder reaching to heaven, and over us
will ascend and descend the angels of God.

Jacob, in this divine narrative, stands for a
large class of men,—those, namely, who know
a little truth in an outward way—some few
facts of religion and faith, and who are in the
effort on the whole to live according to what
they know.   May we not take Jacob as the

A*

representative of the vast majority of religious people in the world at this day? Natural men, we may say, because they think but little and know but little consciously about spiritual things as such. Their life and affections are chiefly in natural and external things. But a man's life and love may be in outward things, —of his family, or his business or his life in the world,—and yet may he be a good man. Everything depends on whether he remembers God or not in his daily life, and tries, in the life that he leads, and that he loves, to keep God's commandments. If he does this, even though his knowledge of divine and interior things be not extensive, and his life as yet a natural life,—that is, a life consisting chiefly in willing and thinking and working in the outward concerns of the body and the world,—yet, if he keep sacredly and religiously in mind the few plain precepts of his religion which he has learned, and tries to let these control his life, he is then such a man as Jacob represents, a man who is in a good life from the truth residing in his natural mind. A man may read a very few books, and forget what little he reads in them, but if he reads one book,—that of God's own Word,—and remembers a few plain precepts of this book, those plain commandments which are the laws of eternal life, of which our God says, "This do and thou shalt live," then has such a man enough of the truth to make him, if he will be, a religious man, yea, a regenerate,— that is, a new-born man, a man so "born again" that he may "enter the kingdom of heaven."

That place whereon Jacob lighted and passed the night, as he journeyed, is just this state or condition of life which I have described,— the state of the natural man as to its dark- ness of mind and the obscurity of its vision of divine things. The night that comes on at the going down of the sun is the doubt and uncer- tainty which comes over our minds at times in the course of our ordinary life, when some old evil desires take hold of us and we are

tempted either to sin and to rebel against our
heavenly Father, or to mistrust his love and
mercy, to reject his Word, to deny his truth,
to question his wisdom, yea, to lose sight of
Him altogether, and to stand alone in our own
dark world, with the sun gone down.

Such extreme states of shaken belief, of
sudden anxieties, and of miserable distrust and
foreboding, are the results of the evils of our
natural mind getting control over us for a
season; but at the beginning of the religious
life we are more or less frequently in such a
night. The world lies in a darkness just
streaked with a little daylight. Our doubts
and our blindness as to spiritual things may
not trouble us much, because we are contented
with the life of the world and its pleasures
and goods; but the soul is nevertheless really
in the dark, it is overtaken by the night, its sun
is hidden. We must tarry; we see no way to
go farther on. For good or bad, in this place
we must tarry all night.

That means until God gives us light again, which He will do if we pray to Him earnestly and really for it.

Meanwhile, what shall a man do?

Shall he give himself up to dissatisfaction, to gloom and discontent and unrest? Shall he say there is nothing certain, nothing strong and sure, nothing but chance or fate? Shall he say there is no happiness to be found in this life? Everywhere is failure and disappointment? That the rewards of a pious, dutiful, religious life are but vain delusions? that the struggle against evil in one's self or in others is after all a vain and hopeless thing? Shall he do this?

Let us see what Jacob did.

Let us note carefully these Divine words: "And he took of the stones of *that place* and put them for his pillows, and lay down in that place to sleep."

Benighted as he was on his way, unable to go farther, to turn right or left, did he think what he might do if he were elsewhere, and vainly stumble on to find a better resting-place? No; he took the stones of that place, just where he was, and made of them a pillow for him to rest upon in that place.

Herein lies the lesson of " Jacob's Pillow." " He took the stones of that place and made himself a pillow, and lay down in that place to sleep." What we want is a pillow in the place where we are,—present help, present security, and rest.

Tired of wandering in the midst of our doubt and darkness, we seek now for some real repose, surety, faith, and strength. If there is a God, if there is a heaven, if there is a communication of our inner life with the better world, and with better, healing, strengthening influences; if faith can cheer us, if charity and good works can strengthen us, if conflict with our besetting sins be really not in vain, we would now know it, and in some strong conviction and unflinching resolve find stability, repose, and peace in our lives. How shall we do this? How shall we, in this place, lay ourselves down in quietness, under the calm and protecting face of Heaven, and find the rest we need for our long life-journey?

Shall we now wish we were something else than what we are, or somewhere else than where we are?

Shall we say to ourselves, If I were only differently situated; if I had this and that incumbrance removed, this or that burden off my shoulders; if, being poor, I was rich; if, being rich and immersed in all the cares of large estates and the responsibilities of business and society,—if I were poor and living a quiet, humble, obscure life; if, being ill, I were well and strong; if, being in vigor of health, and with all the pleasures of a gay and worldly career open before me, I were obliged by ill health to lead a retired and more thoughtful and serious life; if, in a word, I were somewhere else, in some other state, and had other duties placed before me than just these amid which I am, then I could easily combat my evils, could easily. walk in the straight path of happy content and success. But here I am; here has Providence placed me. If I am in doubt, trouble, anxiety, uncertainty, aimlessness, unhappiness, the Lord of my life above me has permitted me to come into this state. He has permitted it to prevent worse evils. He is not unmindful of my condition. He is watching over me, and if I can do as Jacob did, I shall know that from where I lie there is a ladder reaching to heaven, and that his own merciful angels are ascending and descending over where I am.

But to see this, and know this, we must first do as Jacob did; we must in this place lie down, and for our pillow we must take of the stones of this place.

Those who know something of the inner meaning of the words of the Bible, who know what the things there mentioned correspond

to spiritually, will remember that stones correspond to truth,—truth in its plainer, visible,
outward forms, such as we see it in the literal
precepts of God's Word; the truths of the
Ten Commandments for instance, or the truths
which teach us to fight against self-love and all
its sins, to strive to obey God, to love our
fellow-man, to do our duty in that station
where the Divine Providence has placed us.
For to do our duty is to love our neighbor as
ourselves; to love our neighbor is to endeavor
to serve him, to be useful to others both in
natural and spiritual works, to live for others
and not for ourselves. And this we cannot do
except as we remember always that it is God
who makes this our duty, and that the power
and the love to do it can come only from Him.

Now, these are the stones of which we must
make our pillow. The stones of that place
are the duties of to-day. To obey God's
Word in the place or condition where it finds
us, this is to take for our pillow " the stones of

2*

that place." But the stones of one place are not just the same as the stones of some other place. The duties that belong to one person are not just like the duties belonging to another. And the peculiar duties, whether of evil things to be put away, or of good things to be done, these are not the same in one state of our life, one place or period of our life's journey, as are the duties belonging to some other state in our own life. What we have to do is to "take the stones of that place" where we are, the duties or the Divine commands which belong to just that state of mind or condition of life where Providence has permitted us to be placed. We are to take those stones, the divine truth as applying to our present needs, and make of them a pillow whereon we may rest.

What a firm, sure, safe pillow! What a blessed rest! Oh! what a heavenly repose is that for our souls, when we shall see the ladder reaching from the ground, the hard, low ground whereon we have laid ourselves down confiding in God's love and care,—reaching from this ground far up to heaven, and the Lord standing above it, and his angels ascending and descending over us, in their missions of truth and mercy!

A pillow of stones! A hard pillow, do you say? Yes, and often it is indeed a hard one. But except upon that pillow there is no rest for us, no vision of the helping angels, or of our redeeming Lord and heavenly Father. It is a hard pillow in the sense that duties are laborious, our evils hard to resist, our circumstances in life trying, resignation to them difficult,—in a word, in the sense that our selfish, depraved, natural man makes hard and persists in making us think hard any spiritual work, any work of repentance and reformation, any duties of genuine religion, any acting upon the principles of the Church, any ceasing to act on the principles of selfish and worldly love. It is our evils that make the pillow hard. But

when once in the performance of those duties
which are the stones whereon we lie down to
rest, when once we have opened a way for the
light, the comfort, the peace of heavenly
influences within our souls, then how easy do
these duties become, how upon that pillow of
stones does our soul glide away into the
peaceful sleep and the dream of angels!

Reader, as I said at the outset, "our Lord
had no place whereon to lay his head." "Jacob
had a pillow of stones." And you and I and
all men have now, through the Lord's redeeming mercy, a pillow of stones whereon to lie.
The Lord had no place whereon to lay his
head, because there was no truth left in the
Church, or in the world, whereinto his divine
life might flow down to restore the union
of earth to heaven, of lost men to their Creator and Saviour. His Word was falsified and
denied, from beginning to end. Therefore He
came as the Divine, real Word himself, and
was born a man on earth, that the Divine Life,

which is the Father, might be made manifest in
Him and might through Him give light and life
to the world once more.   So He became our
Rock, our Corner-stone, our Foundation, our
Strength, our Rest.   In Him, as the Divine
Word revealed to us, taught us, read by us,
hidden in our hearts, in Him we have the truth
where in every place and condition of our life's
journey we may lay ourselves down and take
our rest.   In his truth, which speaks daily in
our hearts and in our consciences, has He given
us our pillow of stones.   Let us not, heedlessly,
ungratefully, and in our blind complaining, reject this precious gift.

> " Rest of the weary,
>   Joy of the sad ;
> Hope of the dreary,
>   Light of the glad ;
> Home of the stranger,
>   Strength to the end ;
> Refuge from danger,
>   Saviour and Friend !

Pillow where, lying,
　Love rests its head;
Peace of the dying,
　Life of the dead;
When my feet stumble,
　To thee I'll cry,
Crown of the humble,
　Cross of the high:
When my steps wander,
　Over me bend,
Truer and fonder,
　Saviour and Friend!"

II

The Temptation of Eve; or, the Beguilements of the Sensual Man.

And the woman said, The serpent beguiled me, and I did eat.—Gen. III. 13.

IN these words we have the beginning of the sins and the sorrows of our race. Up to this deed of transgression, the Garden of Eden was a paradise, a heaven upon earth. Man's condition was one of celestial innocence; the Divine favor beautified our world and the whole inner and outer life of man. The benediction of the Creator was pronounced upon our earth and all it contained. Man and woman were created in the glorious and perfect image of their Maker, and they were innocent before God and were not ashamed.

For how many years, or centuries, or ages this reign of heavenly innocence and happiness continued, we have no means of learning, nor is it needful to inquire. The important thing to know is, and it is a most grateful and consoling thought, that our race did not begin its history in sin and wickedness; that the dawn of man's life upon earth was fair and radiant with heavenly beauty; and that only after a period perhaps ages in duration did the cloud of evil bring the first gloom upon the human life.

It is commonly said that our first parents sinned, and that evil and its miseries thus began with the human race itself. But this is only an inference drawn from a literal statement in the chapter in Genesis which describes the transgression of Adam and Eve. But already in the first chapter we have the literal statement that God created man male and female: "male and female created he *them;*" and God said, Let *them* have dominion over the lower things of creation.

Thus the man called Adam unquestionably

means the human race, the word itself meaning man as a race. And after this account of
the creation of the race, including male and
female, there follows as a separate history the
account of the Garden of Eden and its inmates.
But no sooner is this account at an end than we
read of Cain going to the land of Nod, taking
a wife and building a city. Now if Adam and
Eve, who transgressed and ate of the forbidden
fruit, were the first and only two human beings
on this earth, then who inhabited the land of
Nod whither their son Cain afterwards went?
And whom could he have taken for a wife?
Who inhabited the city which he built? If the
letter of the Bible is to be adhered to in this
sense, then there were but five persons in existence on our earth, and one of these, the wife
of Cain, could hardly have been at the same
time his sister. Hence, Adam and Eve were at
least not her parents. And, notwithstanding
that there were but five persons living, yet, one
of these already built a city. Such an incon-

sistency only shows very plainly that the names Adam and Eve do not refer to the two first human beings created on our earth, but rather to the whole race, and that what is said of them describes in a figurative manner what took place among the most ancient peoples. We do not here dispute the holy letter of the Scriptures, but we dispute that inference which some have drawn from the letter, and which the letter itself proves to be untenable. What is said of the man and the woman in the Garden of Eden may, indeed, be understood as applying to two persons only; but there is no authority, even in the literal statement of the Bible, for declaring these to be the first and only parents of our race. In a figurative sense we may properly speak of them as such, knowing that Adam means man and Eve woman, and knowing also that what is recorded of them in the Holy Word is, when spiritually understood, a most perfect and truthful history of what occurred in the interior or spiritual life of those ancient peoples from whom the nations of the earth now living are descended.

But knowing as the church does at this day from revelation that the Holy Word is divine, and treats therefore of spiritual things under the clothing and imagery of natural things, we shall look to the spiritual contents of this history of the fall of our race for that spiritual and saving knowledge which the Lord designs to offer us through his Word. He has spoken these things concerning the creation of the world and the sin of our race in a parable; but He does not design that we should remain ever in the parable, the enigma, only; and at length that time has come when, by unfolding to the church the spiritual sense of the sacred Scriptures, "He speaks to us no longer in proverbs," and He tells us those many things which the minds of men, in past ages, were not ready to receive. In a word, according to the spiritual sense of these first chapters of Gene-

sis, the history of the creation of the world and
Adam describes really the new creation, the
regeneration of man's soul from being chaos .
and darkness to attaining the image and like-
ness of God.   The Garden of Eden is an
image in natural things of the celestial and
blessed state of the human race while yet in
their primitive innocence and order.   By Adam
is meant this celestial or heavenly mind as to
its rational or intellectual faculty ; by woman,
or Eve, is meant that sense of one's own self-
hood, or distinct existence, which comes from
our being a free agent, capable of leading ourselves or being led by another.   This self-
hood of man, denoted by Eve, when filled with
innocence from the Lord, and when freely
determined to follow the Lord, is that which
makes man's spiritual nature complete, and
enables him to follow the Lord from love and
choice, instead of being compelled thereto.
From this heavenly and better self man serves
the Lord, and is yet in the enjoyment of the

highest freedom. He does not act, like a machine, solely from a power communicated from without, but as if from his own self, as the motive power, although this very self-hood, or free will itself, is equally the gift of God.

When man from this heaven-inspired self wills freely to obey the Lord and live according to the Divine laws, he is enjoying the freedom of heaven itself; for the very blessedness and liberty of heaven consists solely in the harmony between it and those laws which have their origin in the infinite love and perfect wisdom of the Lord.

So long as this seemingly independent selfhood of man looks up to the Lord and desires to be wholly governed and led by Him, so long is it innocent; and even self-love, being subordinate to the love of God, and being itself the condition of man's freely loving others, is so far good and holy. And this is what is meant by the innocence in which Adam and his Eve were before their transgression. They

3*

were not ashamed. No! for as yet there was
nothing sinful in this self-hood,—this free will
of man; the Lord kept it in innocence. But
when man, from his independent self-hood,
began to look downward to the things of
nature and the appetites of the senses for
motives of conduct, then this same self-hood
was the instrument or medium of his being
tempted, and of his committing sin. Man's
free, voluntary nature, the moment it turns
away from the Lord and the guidance of the
interior motives of love and faith, and looks
out to the world and its attractions, that moment it makes a way for evil to come into and
darken and poison the human life. For man's
external and sensuous life should be controlled
by the inner, and not the outer man. So long
as the Lord rules from within, through love
and faith, so long is the selfish nature of man
kept subordinate and made useful and conducive to his true freedom and happiness. For
to be free and happy is to live according to

God's truth. But so soon as the external and corporeal nature of man is ruled by the things of the world, then it assumes a power which brings the internal or heavenly man into subjection; the love of self and the love of the world become predominant, and the whole life becomes gradually more and more sensual and earthly.

The fall of man consists, therefore, in this sin: that his self-hood, signified by the woman, by virtue of its freedom, which was God's holy gift, turned away from the inner guidance of God to the outer seductions of the senses and the world; and thus self-love, from being the innocent medium by which man could serve God and his neighbor, became the medium by which he not only served, but became a slave to, the world and to the evil passions and miserable lusts of his carnal nature.

The woman said, "The serpent beguiled me, and I did eat."

The ancients, when they desired to represent

a quality of the human mind, did not compare it to an animal or other object, but called it directly by the name of the animal or thing which corresponded to it. The same practice is adhered to in much of the writings of the Holy Word. Thus is our Lord named by the prophets and by the Evangelists the lion, and also the lamb. The lion evidently represents his Divine power; the lamb his perfect innocence. So our Lord Himself, speaking of Herod, calls him "that fox," by which He would indicate his selfish, human cunning, as opposed to the heavenly wisdom of love and faith. Now the serpent, spoken of in our text as tempting the woman, is also the representative of a quality in the human mind; and it is easy to see what this quality is.

The serpent here mentioned is the sensual principle in man. It lies close to the earth, as the sensual things of the mind are closely connected with the body. Those who depend upon the evidence of the senses alone, whose confidence is only in material, tangible things, whose whole mind is, as it were, in their eyes, mouth, and organs of touch, whose reasoning is only from sensuous or visible things,—such persons are called serpents in the Holy Scriptures, and their natures do so truly correspond to the serpent that the creature itself may better represent the quality than any verbal definition depict it. The serpent is wary, cunning, circumspect, swift, agile, deceitful, and armed with a deadly sting. It may properly symbolize, therefore, qualities both good and bad. For prudence and acuteness and careful discrimination are very desirable qualities, and necessary for all to have who would walk safely the ways of this world. The intelligence which man derives from science and from experience with men, all those good and useful things which we acquire through the use of the bodily senses,—these find also their symbol in the serpent. These are a necessary part of every man's nature, even the most pure and heavenly;

B*

consequently our Lord warned his disciples to be wise as serpents; and the serpent lifted up in the wilderness was the divinely-chosen prophecy of our Lord's suffering upon the cross, and the elevation and glorification in divine purity of the very lowest principles of that flesh and nature which He put on in this world.

And it is easy to see that while man's rational and voluntary nature are devoted to following the heavenly dictates of love and faith, then the bodily senses and their knowledge will only tend to the growth of heavenly intelligence in the soul; for all external knowledge and experience will be made use of to high and spiritual ends. But let the love of self and of the world for their own sake get the mastery; let not the inmost soul, but the life of the body, be consulted; then is the evidence of the senses brought in to contradict that of faith; then are the pleasures of the world and the gratification of natural desires more de-

lightful than those of the inner life; then self-
love leads the reason, and the senses lead self-
love, and the power and the cunning of the
senses and sensual things are able to lead man
wholly away from the freedom of heaven into
the bondage of hell.   Thus it is that the man
said, "The woman beguiled me;" and the
woman said, "The serpent beguiled me, and I
did eat."

It is wonderful when we reflect what are the
four characters introduced in this scene in the
Garden of Eden.   They are the Lord, man,
woman, and the serpent.   It is a perfect picture of the human mind at all times.   That
scene is repeated again and again in the
interior life of us all, whether we be consciously aware of it or not.   The Lord is in
the inmost, in the highest, heavenly degree of
the mind, speaking by his Holy Spirit, warning
us by the voice of conscience, moving us
secretly, restraining us gently, leading us, if
possible, in the heavenly way.   Beneath, or

next in order to this celestial plane, through
which the Lord exerts the influence of his
Holy Spirit, is the rational or spiritual plane
of the mind, represented by Adam. Beneath
this again is the external man in which one
realizes consciously one's self-hood, in which
one seems to think, to feel, to act, to live of
one's self. This is Eve, the woman. And
beneath this plane still is the most external or
sensual degree of the mind, which is closely
connected with the body and the outer world,
and which is made up of thoughts, knowledges, and appetites, directly connected with
the bodily senses. This plane of the mind, or
of the human life, is the serpent that is ever
beguiling the woman to eat of the tree of
the knowledge of good and evil, and to be as
God. The true heavenly order of the mind is
that wherein the Lord not only rules and provides, but is looked up to as the way and the
source of all blessing and happiness. The
rational faculty filled with love and faith then

leads the lower, selfish nature to look upward to pure and heavenly pursuits and delights, to serve not self for the sake of self, but to live for the delights of charity; and the lower, the sensual mind, brings in all its treasures of seeing and hearing, and all the experiences of the outer life, to prove the goodness of God and his wisdom, and to enrich the mind with materials for useful and happy labor. Controlled by a pure love of God, and illumined by the light of heaven, the reason directs the external will, and thus brings the senses into subjection to the laws of true order and usefulness. Those things which pertain to man's happiness and his relations to God, and also the mysteries of the future life, man, while in this orderly condition, views from an interior perception. The substance of the spiritual life, its reality and its happiness, are revealed to him from within. The world without corresponds to and fulfills all this inward experience. Man is content thus to obey the Lord, to be depend-

ent on Him, and to know and believe that which
is thus interiorly verified to him.

But when man begins to desire to depend on
himself, and to be led by himself, then he appeals
to self for evidence of duty, of right and wrong,
of happiness and unhappiness, and self looks
out to the world and its sensuous experiences,
and thus the whole order of life is inverted.
The celestial or heavenly mind is made subordinate, and the sensual mind is placed supreme.
The voice which dictates and teaches is now no
longer the voice of God, but the voice of the
serpent. The delight of man is no longer in
being led by the Lord, and feeling one's de-
pendence upon Him, and confiding in his revealed truth for all knowledge of duty and
of happiness, but is rather in touching that
forbidden fruit which the serpent holds out, in
appealing to the senses and the world for a
test of what is good and not good, in being
one's own master and one's own teacher, in
verifying by visible and tangible proof the

things of faith and revelation, thus, in a word, in "eating of the fruit of the tree of knowledge, and in being as God, knowing good and evil."

It was in this inversion of the mind that sin, disorder, and all the sorrows of the world had their beginning. It was in looking to self rather than to the Lord, and consulting the senses and earthly science rather than Divine revelation for the rule of faith and of duty. The story is ever the same to this day, the sin is the same, the miserable consequences are the same. Man's soul, subjecting reason to self-love, and self-love to the dictates of sensual pleasure and sensual evidence, is become a slave to the world and the victim to its deceits. The love of self and of the world has for its inevitable result, if cultivated and willingly indulged, to make a man believe in himself and not in the Lord and his Word, and to suppose that what he cannot apprehend sensuously and scientifically has no existence. Men thus become, says Swedenborg, "altogether evil and false, and thus see all things perversely; they regard evil as good, and good as evil; falses as truths, and truths as falses; realities as nothing, and nothing as everything. They call hatred, love; darkness, light; death, life. They are denominated in the Word, the lame and the blind."

This, then, is the self-love of man which, turned away from the Lord, and relying on itself or on the evidence of the senses rather than on the truths of revelation, and following the enticements of the senses rather than the dictates of religion, is infernal and accursed.

Look out upon the world, and behold the vices, the foolish and insane pleasures, the wars, the ruin and iniquity in which men do in our day run riot. Listen to what the so-called learned say and write, turning God's Holy Word into ridicule and a lie, and resolving the Deity itself into a mere reflection of our own miserable humanity,—and then say if the serpent has not beguiled the woman, and the

woman the man, and they together eaten the
forbidden fruit and become as gods, knowing
good and evil. The rejection of faith and
contempt of God's Word is proving in our
day the truth of that warning word of the
Lord: "In the day that ye eat thereof, ye shall
surely die." For, says Swedenborg again, "a
desire to investigate the mysteries of faith by
the senses and science is the cause of the fall
of every church; for hence come not only
false opinions, but also evils of life.

. . . "Those who consult the senses and
science respecting what is to be believed, not
only precipitate themselves into doubt, but
also into denial and thus into darkness, and
into every kind of cupidity. For when they
believe the false, they practice the false. And
when they believe there is nothing spiritual
and celestial, they believe that only the corporeal and worldly exists, and, accordingly, they
love what is of self and the world; and, hence,
from this falsity come lusts and evils. At this

4*

day the evil is much greater than at former times, because men can now confirm the incredulity of the senses by scientific reasonings unknown to the ancients, which have given birth to an indescribable degree of darkness at which men would be astounded did they know its extent!"—[*Arcana Cœlestia*, 232, 233.]

The serpent of our sensual nature is ever beguiling us to taste the pleasures of sin, and to rely upon external rather than internal evidence as to what is good, enjoyable, and enduring; and if we yield to self-love, we shall, before we are aware, have lost our faith in the truths of God's Word, and shall be able no longer to bring our perplexities and our doubt to that sure and final arbiter, but shall be left to be tossed and driven about by the fluctuating passions and whims of a worldly heart and infidel mind.

Faith dies within us the moment we place sensual evidence and sensual good over Divine revelation and the duties of religion. And as faith dies the soul dies.

Driven from Paradise, and shut out from its pure delights by our actual sins, let us look to Him who, according to the prophecy, has come to bruise the serpent's head, and to open those blessed gates once more to a sinful and sorrowful world. He has said to the children of men, "Come unto me, all ye that labor, and I will give you rest." He is the way, the truth, and the life. He it is who, like the serpent in the wilderness, being Himself "lifted up," is drawing unto Himself all those who believe in Him and do the work of repentance.

> " Thou strong and loving Son of man,
> 　　Redeemer from the bonds of sin,
> ' Tis Thou the living spark dost fan
> 　　That sets the breast on fire within.
>
> "Thou openest heaven once more to men,
> 　　The soul's true home, thy kingdom, Lord,
> And I can trust and hope again
> 　　And feel myself akin to God.

"In Thee I find a nobler birth,
 A glory o'er the world I see,
And Paradise returns to earth,
 And blooms again for us in Thee."

III.

Noah's Dove; or, the Soul set Free.

And he stayed yet other seven days; and sent forth the dove, which returned not again unto him any more.—
Gen. viii. 12.

THE students of the Bible and of nature have had much to say about the Flood, querying as to when and where it occurred, and how widely it prevailed. I do not know that they have advanced much beyond the plain narrative given in Genesis; and if they had established all the natural facts concerning it to their own and everybody's satisfaction, I do not know that we would be spiritually much wiser than we may be on reading this simple narration in God's Holy Word. But it is quite certain that if men would give an equal amount of attention and care to the study of that Flood which is now and at all times prevailing in some degree over their mental

45

world; if they would watch the rise and fall
of its waters, and be on the lookout for
its mountain-tops, and for the happy rest in
Ararat, the mountain of Light; then would this
be no longer a vain study of what is merely
temporary and local, but a pursuit of what
belongs to the immortal, spiritual life of our
race. This would be a study indeed of the
Bible account of the Flood in its genuine and
true sense. For all things in the outer world
are pictures of things in the soul's world. And
the Bible everywhere, in relating what seem
to be natural occurrences, is describing really
the things which take place in our souls, or in
the inner, spiritual world. So it is with the
story of the Flood. The waters of the Flood
are the temptations and desolations which come
over the immortal souls of men. The earth
which is covered is the depraved will, with its
evil lusts and passions; for over these rise
higher and higher the waters of conflict and
temptation.

The ark, with its contents, is the church in the soul; that is, the remnant of whatever is good and holy and saving preserved by the Divine mercy from entire destruction, laid up within the conscience, or the higher part of man, there to be the means of his enduring, unhurt, the time of tribulation, and of his coming finally to the place of his soul's rest and salvation. All those who are drowned by the Flood are those who have not the elements of the church in them, who have not preserved a good and pure conscience intact even amid the rising waters of false persuasions and evil seduction. These are drowned; their souls are carried away to hell by the overwhelming tide of evils and false persuasions, the cunning voices of secret, sinful desire, the constant drawing of evil habits too long indulged in.

But those in the ark are saved. They are not a single family only, but they are the thousands of faithful souls of whom Noah and his family are the symbol or representative. They are

all who are of the spiritual church,—the church
of faith; they are all, that is, who have the
church with its faith and its charity in their souls.
These are borne safely over the waters of the
flood; these rise as the waters rise; these see
the old, the corrupted, and evil world disappear
before their eyes, and at length see again the
mountain-tops as of a new earth, and behold
over them the rainbow as in new heavens of
light and beauty and everlasting peace.

The first idea that comes to the mind of a
child or grown person, in reading of the Flood
and the ark, is, no doubt, that it was a fine
thing to be Noah, floating securely in the ark
over all the wide waste of waters under which
his fellow-men had perished, and to have with
him there his own family, and a pair of all the
fowl and cattle and creeping things.

Well, it was indeed a good thing, but not
pleasant after our earthly way of judging.
It was the means of salvation, but its way a
hard and tiresome way. Noah longed to see

the waters abate and the land appear again. He longed for the dry land, the blooming fields, the wide, free earth, wherein to range abroad. His ark was a prison; the endless, dreary waste of waters was like a vast wall, shutting in his steps, his gaze, his whole life, to the narrow world of self. The heavens above were dark with the clouds of rain. He longed again for the sun, the smell of the earth, the sound of the cattle in the pastures, and the pursuits of the busy, homely life.

The landsman who has made a long voyage at sea, knows how refreshing and heart-restoring is the first sight of land; and when the land-gales bring him the sweet odors of woods and the sounds of the lowing cattle, or of the farmer's scythe, or of the church-bell ringing in a distant hamlet, his bosom swells with a new and nameless emotion. He thanks God, whose are the seas and who made them, that he has been preserved while upon deep waters; but again he thanks God, whose hands did form the dry land, that on the dry land is his home and that the harbor is nigh.

Thus Noah longed to go forth from the ark. He rejoiced when, at the end of forty days, he "opened the window of the ark he had made" and beheld the tops of the mountains. And he sent out first a raven, "which went forth to and fro, until the waters were dried up." And then he sent forth a dove from him, to see if the waters were abated. But the dove found no rest for the sole of her foot, and returned unto him into the ark, for the waters were on the face of the whole earth; and he put forth his hand and took her, and pulled her unto him in the ark. And he stayed yet other seven days; and again he sent forth the dove out of the ark; and the dove came in to him in the evening; and, lo, in her mouth was an olive-leaf, plucked off: so Noah knew that the waters were abated from off the earth. And he stayed yet other seven days; and again he sent forth the dove, which returned not again unto him any more.

The story of the ark, of the long and dreary confinement, of the raven and the dove sent forth, and of the dove's finding at last a rest for the sole of her foot and returning no more, —this is at once a beautiful and a true story of the life of the soul which is being regenerated. We have not here an allegory merely that we can apply at random to anything we wish to illustrate, but an accurate history of those states of the soul which do actually succeed each other in the course of spiritual birth and progress. Let us for a moment reverently and carefully explore the inner meaning of this wondrous narrative. The recollection of these sacred mysteries of the Divine wisdom hidden in the depths of the Word of God, of which we may obtain, indeed, but a poor and imperfect glimpse, may be in some future hour a source of strength and consolation to the soul.

I have called the life in the ark an imprison-
ment, and, therefore, said that it was no pleasant condition to be in, after our worldly way
of thinking. But it is the true and only condition of security in the time when the floods
of infernal evil are sweeping over our soul's
world. The way of life is elsewhere called a
straight and narrow way into which few enter.
So with the ark, it is a narrow place for the
abode of the soul. We seek rather the free,
open land; and our efforts toward this life of
true spiritual liberty are described by the
sending forth of the dove three times from
the ark.

This, then, is to be borne in mind, that the
ark represents that bondage to which we
are committed; that involuntary confinement
within the laws of our religion, while the
world's temptations surge about the soul, and
when our first step from the limits which our
conscience has set up is a step into the deep
and perilous waters of evil and the soul's

ruin. The mountain-tops appearing are as the dawn of faith, which promises us freedom at last, which says the land is near,—that good land where we may go in and out and find pasture,—that is, where we shall live freely, where, our hearts being impelled by the love of what is good and in accordance with the holy will of God, we may act out those impulses of the renewed will, and find in the service of God the only real and true liberty.

And we send forth the dove, as did Noah, every time we explore our lives by the light of the Divine Word, to see if genuine, unselfish goodness and the truth which we inwardly honor and are compelling ourselves to obey, with much difficulty, perhaps, and with frequent failure, if these, the elements of the church within, are taking root and actually growing up in our lower and external man; if the low and brutal passions and desires of the flesh, if selfish and unbelieving worldliness are giving way in reality to sentiments of true charity, to the higher and angelic affections for what is purely true and good.

In the narrative it is said that after forty days the mountain-tops appeared, and Noah opened the window and looked out; and he first sent a raven out, which went forth to and fro. It is not said that the raven came back. We are not told where the raven rested, but it did not come back. But the dove which Noah sent forth came back, finding no rest for the sole of her foot.

And it is so with every one who, after a long period of his life, spent amid the tumults of temptation, of inward conflict and struggle between the evil desires of the heart and the religious restraints of the conscience, begins at last to behold the reality of a spiritual faith, to feel assured of final victory, to believe that God's truth, firmly adhered to in the conscience, will at last be the stronger, and will enable him to master his evil inclinations. The waters seem to abate; the dawn appears; the moun-

tain-tops are seen. With the eye of faith and
trust the penitent and long-tried soul looks out
upon the dreary waste of this world's life.

Through the opened window of the soul the
light of heaven pours in ; a sense of rest and
hope and confidence comes over him. The
flood is past; now he will go forth bold and
strong upon the new and better life.

But it is only a raven that is sent out to
explore the land,—a raven which flies to and
fro, and comes not back. The raven is a bird
of darkness, an image of the false imaginings
that spring from the evil heart. So long as
the will is not purified of its evil desires and
likings, the thoughts which it puts forth are but
false and deceitful. The survey of life, made
by the first dim light of faith, is apt to be
a false and deceptive one. The life of religion looks easy and practicable enough, but
there lies selfishness at the bottom of our
motives after all. This our religion, so readily
put on, is but a cloak to hide our real infidel

nature from the world and those whose judgment we fear, or whose favor we seek; and
our faith thus outwardly professed, is but the
flatterer of some selfish love,. some hidden
pride, some secret desire to be rewarded for
our goodness in another world, to be thought
better than our neighbors in this. But this is
not the rest and peace and liberty of the
spiritual life. This is not the life of genuine
religion brought down to the natural will,
entering into all the motives and affections of
external man. The raven flies to and fro.
There is still unrest, still the seeking and not
finding, still the unsatisfied longing for real
freedom and final repose. The internal vision
is obscured by the false ideas of the unregenerate reason. The old law of the flesh—the
notion that this and that is good, and to be
sought after, because the natural will desires
it—still asserts its sway. The false principle,
represented by the raven, although finding nowhere rest, and bringing no real peace and

quiet to the soul, continues to invade even
the believing mind so long as the earth is
submerged; that is, so long as the natural will
is still inspired with its inherited affections of
evil. Happy is he whose first glance at his
life from the window of faith sees fluttering
about this bird of falsehood, this omen of evil;
for he then knows that the heart is not pure,
the mind is not full of light, but that he has
still to rid himself of much that is evil and
false. Happy for him that the raven goes to
and fro, and comes not back again; the ques-
tionings, the doubts, the anxieties of mind
caused by the presence of this conflicting
element of unbelief and falsity, will only tend,
in the end, to purify the mind and establish it
the more surely in the truths of saving faith.

But the dove is next sent forth. The dove
is the spirit of goodness and truth, going
forth from the faith which is in man's interior
nature. The Lord resides in the inmost soul;
it is from his presence there that man has con-

c*

science or preserves any remnant of goodness and truth and can exercise any faith. In this plane of the life, signified by sending forth the dove from the ark, it is the Lord that in reality gives us the knowledge to detect our sins and the spirit to overcome them. The dove being the symbol of all that is innocent and holy in our faith, its going forth naturally typifies the desire on the part of the holy principle in the inner man to implant itself in the outer man, to be made actual in the daily life. It is a desire that the will of God, as understood and revered in the interior mind, may descend and be carried out in the life of the body in all the lower and outermost details of man's life in the world; that thus the Divine petition may be fulfilled, "Thy will be done on earth as it is in heaven."

But what is the result of this desire on the part of the faithful soul thus to bring its religion down to the external, daily life? The dove goes forth indeed, but it returns again,

"having found no rest for the sole of her foot."
Thus, in that ground of the natural will, there
is still no room for the heavenly principles of
goodness and truth. Religion is still only a
thing of belief, an exalted state of thought and
feeling occasionally experienced in the soul,
but as yet having no real rest and basis in the
external, actual conduct of life. No ; leaving
the intellect, the memory, the occasional excite-
ment of the purer and more refined emotions
of the soul out of sight,—for in these such like
religion of faith finds its abode,—and coming
down to the body with its passions, the natural
heart with its tastes and desires, its purposes
and plans, its hopes and its ambitions, we shall
find little room there for the real influence
of spiritual motives, of genuine love of goodness and truth for their own sake, or for the
sake of the Holy Father and giver of them to
the soul. It is not that a man is leading a
voluntary evil life, for he has already for a long
time perhaps been ruled in his outward actions

by the dictates of his conscience; but still this life of outward goodness and order is discordant to his heart's real affections; and therefore it is said that in the ground, that is, in the affections of the will, the dove, or the holy spirit of faith, finds no rest for the sole of her foot.

But another seven days go by, another week, or spiritual season of trial; and again the seventh, a holy day of rest, is come. Advanced through renewed temptations and newly-gained victories to a higher state of life, again the holy things of religion seek escape from the narrow chambers of the inner mind into the broad realm of the actual life.

And now the dove, sent forth again, returns in the even-time, and, lo, an olive-leaf pluckt off. This, the olive-leaf, is the first harbinger of peace, the promise of the holy fruit of religion which shall yet be borne on the redeemed and enlivened soil of the heart. The olive-tree is the good of charity: the leaf is the truth which teaches this goodness. The olive-leaf brought back by the dove at even-time is the first dawn of that perception of truth which comes from good affections in the heart. For there are two sorts of truth known in men : The truths learned and retained in the intellect, and the truths that tell themselves, as it were, out of the depths of pure religious love and actual charity of daily life.

The latter truths are called perceptions. They are the highest consciousness of truth we have. They are like the voice of the Holy Spirit speaking softly and secretly in the inner man. When thus we begin to know the truth from the love of that goodness which the truth teaches, then we may know that land is near; that the long, wearisome journey over temptation's rough waters is well-nigh ended; that our foot shall soon find rest on the broad lands of free and peaceful and happy living.

Yea, and when yet another seven days are ended, when the last trials necessary for the soul's purification and victory over its evils are undergone to the end, and the blessed Sabbath of heavenly rest dawns upon us, then shall we send forth the dove, never to return again.

The dove shall find at last its rest upon the refreshed and blooming land; the waters shall have left the earth; the fountains of the abyss shall be dried up. With our wills cleansed by the waters of temptation from every evil thing and ready to bear the fruits of our faith in the lowest as in the highest relations and duties of life, we shall go forth at length from the place of bondage into the broad land of spiritual freedom. No longer shall the gulf of the evil and the false threaten us on every side; no longer shall the infernal abyss send forth its wretched crew to infest our souls, to overwhelm us with their false and deathly persuasions. We shall have learned to live in and by the truth of God's Word; and the truth shall make us free.

Such is the liberty, such the peace of heaven. Is it not worth the long and tedious voyage

to come to such a land at last? Is it not
the wiser part here to govern our lives by
the straight though often trying and irksome
rule of our religion, seeing that thus only shall
we rise above those desolating evils and fatal
delusions under which so many souls have
gone down, than to mistake for freedom the
bondage to our evil passions and appetites,
those chains which Satan is ever trying to
forge around our souls?

The true freedom in this life is the render-
ing of careful service and obedience to God's
holy laws. This may be involuntary, and thus
arduous and difficult, and the way of indul-
gence seem the only broad, free way. But
all that makes God's service arduous is the
unwilling, the unconverted heart. When the
heart's affections are for heavenly things,
when the heart is ready to enjoy the happiness
of heaven, then will its delight be in the law
of the Lord; and we shall walk at liberty
seeking his precepts.

IV

Melchizedek's Oblation; or, the Sacrament of the Supper of the Lord.

And Melchizedek king of Salem brought forth bread and wine : and he was the priest of the most high God.— Gen. xiv. 18.

MANY centuries have passed over the earth since the event here described took place. And yet in this simply but forcibly portrayed picture we see the true pattern of that which to-day is done before our own eyes. Now, too, upon the altars of our churches, are the bread and wine brought forth by the Lord's priest and offered for the blessing of every soul that, like Abraham, comes home victorious from the battle with the enemy. What sublime meaning lay hid in that bread and wine brought forth by the king of Salem and offered unto Abraham, a refreshment and a blessing in the midst of the arduous conflicts of his life! Long ages passed away, and in the same city of Salem again are those wondrous symbols, bread and wine, brought forth for the refreshment of man. Again is it Melchizedek, the true King of Righteousness, yea, it is Salem's rightful and eternal King, who now on the night of his own betrayal, after eating the passover with his disciples, takes bread and wine and distributes to them, saying of the bread, "this is my Body," and of the wine, "this is my Blood." And so doing, He, who is verily a Priest forever after the order of Melchizedek, enjoins upon his human followers the perpetual offering of the same bread and wine, saying, "This do in remembrance of me!"

And now, when we see before us, upon the Lord's table, the same sacred symbols consecrated by the worship of ages, forever distinguished from all other created substance by being chosen by our blessed Saviour as the emblems of his own Divine Body and Blood,

when, in obedience to his solemn command,
we come into the presence of our eternal Priest
and King to receive, under the figure of these
material elements, that heavenly refreshment
of which our souls are in need, and reflect how,
before the abiding statutes of our Divine religion, the ages, the nations, the monuments of
earth pass away and are as nothing, shall we
not recognize in this most holy Sacrament that
which is forever above man's devising, that
which could only have been conceived by Him
whose eye beholds eternity, "whose commandments stand fast for ever and ever, and are
done in truth and uprightness"? Yea, well
may we exclaim in the presence of this perpetual memorial of the Divine mercy, in the
presence of those symbols which for many
ages prophesied, and which for evermore shall
recall, the Divine incarnation, the eternal Word
made flesh, the Bread of heaven come down to
be the food of man,—"The works of the Lord
are great, sought out of all them that have

pleasure therein. He sent redemption unto
his people; He hath commanded his covenant
forever; holy and reverend is his name!"

> "Therefore we, before Him bending,
>   This great Sacrament revere ;
> Types and shadows have their ending,
>   For the newer rite is here ;
> Faith, our outward sense befriending,
>   Makes our inward vision clear."

In Melchizedek's offering of bread and wine
we behold an early type of the Holy Supper of
the Christian Church. The occasion and the
circumstance of this offering will, therefore, be,
in a figurative manner, analogous to those
states of worship which are proper to the
celebration by the Christian of this most holy
solemnity.

Abraham, we read, returned from his wars
with King Chedorlaomer, who had conquered,
together with many other lands, also Sodom,
the land wherein Abraham's brother Lot dwelt,
and had taken Lot captive. Abraham returned

victorious, having liberated his brother and destroyed this invading king and his host. Now, as he returns to his home, it is written, "And Melchizedek king of Salem brought forth bread and wine: and he was the priest of the most high God." And he blessed Abraham.

We may behold in this history of Abraham a twofold representative. On the one hand, Abraham may be regarded as the prophetic type of our Saviour, and all that is recorded of Abraham is, in its spiritual meaning, a description of the interior life of our Lord in assuming and glorifying his humanity. It is to this interior reference to Himself, contained in the spiritual sense of the Old Testament, that our Lord referred when He said, "Search the Scriptures, for they testify of me," and also when He explained unto his disciples, in the books of Moses, the Prophets, and the Psalms, "things concerning Himself." But our Saviour's life in the humanity was itself a pattern of what ours

should be in becoming truly his followers.
Therefore the spiritual things contained in
Abraham's history may also have reference to
the experience of all men alike in becoming
regenerate.

In the midst of a life of war and disquietude
behold, then, a season of temporary victory and
rest, a peaceful return to one's home, the
greeting of one who is both priest and king,
and the refreshment and blessing tendered by
his hand in the name of the most high God.
Can we not in this outline behold some dearly-
remembered scene out of the life we have
lived? Or may we not at least have this
before us as that which is promised to every
Christian by the Divine mercy and wisdom
which ordained the sacrament of the Holy
Supper? For what is this but a feast of refreshment and blessing by the way-side of a
weary and toilsome life? When do we appre-
ciate this so fully as after a season of bitter
temptations and internal warfare? Who alone

is it who meets us at the gates of Salem, the eternal city of Peace? Who stills the conflict of the soul and fills our hearts with new vigor, with happy hopes and fresh courage, but the same Giver of all Peace, the true Melchizedek, the King of Righteousness, the eternal Priest?

Like Abraham, we have our battles to fight. We must expect at times to have the quiet, the happy security of our inner life disturbed, and to have to go down to fight the invaders of Sodom and Gomorrah, where our brother is being taken captive. In other words, we must endure temptations from the things of the lower and outer man. We are drawn into all kinds of snares and enticements by the appetites and the persuasions of the senses and the reasonings of the depraved will. This lower and sensual degree of the nature is that brother Lot which we are to rescue. With the light of Divine truth and with all the high motives of our religion we must go down into the fray. Faith, perseverance, self-denial, and brotherly

love must be brought into hand-to-hand conflict with doubt and denial of God and religion,
with a weak, self-indulgent, self-excusing morality, with a mighty, almost irresistible impulse
to have one's own way, to accomplish one's own
purposes, let what will stand between. For
our better nature, our conscience, the seat of
our faith, and of our truly good and upright
motives, so far as we have any, stands in the
relation of a brother to the lower, carnal, and
self-willed part of our being. Abraham is the
representative of the internal, and consequently
the higher and heavenly plane of the mind.
Lot, that of the external, the worldly, or natural
plane. The war of Abraham for the deliverance
of Lot is, therefore, only a figure descriptive
of every conflict which goes on in the human
heart between the higher and the lower motives
and principles of conduct. Conscience, revelation, religion, against appetite, infidelity, self-in-
dulgence ; the angels of heaven arrayed against
Satan ; the spirit warring against the flesh.

Nor as a man advances in Christian life does this conflict, this occasional anxiety and distress of soul, become less intense and severe, but rather more so. Like the young warrior, the better he is skilled in the use of arms the farther he is sent to the front into the heat of the conflict. Many souls pass through the world in a state of sluggish sleep, hardly knowing at all what that temptation of spirit, what that tribulation is through which man enters the kingdom of heaven. They purposely dull their hearts that they may not feel the cuts of remorse. They blind their eyes that they may not see, and make themselves deaf that they may not hear. They are like Lot in his captured land of Sodom, without a brother Abraham dwelling at Hebron who may come down and rescue him.

But if the Christian's conflict is more severe as he advances in the life of religion, if temptations multiply, and, in growing more interior and refined and subtle, become thereby all the more intense in their power and insidious in their attacks, on the other hand he is supplied with ever-increasing strength from the Almighty defender and protector of the faithful; he is nearer to the Lord, and receives more immediately and constantly the inflowings of the Divine life.

In whatever resistance we can offer to an evil enticement, in whatever endurance, patience, courage, and hope we maintain in seasons of intense anguish of spirit, and when we are tempted by a thousand things, within and without, to give way to despair and tears and the overwhelming sorrows of the heart, in our every conflict with evil in whatever form, the Lord is present with us, and gives to us all the power we have to resist, to endure, and to overcome. He is never nearer, never more abundantly affording us the goodness and the truth we need, than just when we are in our most grievous temptations, when we seem most forsaken and alone. But these secret affec-

tions of good and truth, the genuine love and
faith we receive from Him, the source of all
our soul's life and strength,—these at such
times are not perceived in us in their own
quality. Coming at once into conflict with
the evils so violently roused within us, they
add only to the distress and confusion of our
minds, even as the arrival of fresh troops on
the field of battle, although the harbinger of
final victory and peace, does yet at first only
make the contest more fierce and desperate.

But it is of the Divine Providence that this
inner strife between good and evil should not
have to be constantly maintained, and that man
should enjoy occasional seasons of seeming
victory and peaceful repose. Like the regu-
larly recurring Sabbaths, the days of rest, and
like the cities of refuge set apart in times of
old, wherein a man, whatever wickedness he
may have done, was for a time secure from his
pursuers, so do the occasional intervals of
peaceful, quiet, harmonious life serve to re-

fresh, enliven, and encourage the soul of man. In these seasons of rest a man is not rid of or cleansed from his old evils, but the affections and thoughts of evil are, as it were, put to sleep in his mind; they give over for awhile their combat against what is good, heavenly, and peaceful; they cease to trouble and torment the soul with their innumerable temptations; though not wholly conquered, they do for a season keep the peace. And it is in those times that man feels the blessings of the Divine presence, and learns something of the nature of that heavenly food with which the Lord is constantly nourishing our immortal souls. Though in reality no nearer now than in more troubled and unquiet hours, though affording us no more directly the food and aid we need than when we are in the midst of the fray, still, now in the hour of tranquil and exalted rest the Lord reveals Himself more clearly to us as the bringer of peace and of every spiritual blessing, and we know the near-

ness of heaven not by the discord between it
and the evils of our hearts, but by the sweet
harmony into which it draws all our better feel-
ings and thoughts. So, indeed, at the gate of
Salem meets the soul after temptations its true
Priest Melchizedek, both King and Priest, who
brings forth bread and wine and blesses it in
the Divine name. This true eternal Priest, who
alone can refresh and bless the soul, is the Lord
Jesus Christ. He is called.the Priest after the
order of Melchizedek, for Melchizedek, who
is both Priest and King, signifies the giver and
dispenser of all heavenly goodness and of all
heavenly truth. And those two elements of
spiritual life—goodness and truth, or love and
wisdom—are what make up the food of the
soul; they are the spiritual bread and wine
with which the soul is refreshed by the Lord at
the gate of Salem, the city of peace.

Salem, afterwards called Jerusalem, and for
evermore to be known to the Church as the New
Jerusalem, means "Peace"; and Abraham's

return to Salem is the soul's entrance after a time of spiritual temptation into a state of heavenly peace and consolation. Melchizedek means "the king of righteousness," and he is king of Salem; therefore he represents the Lord as ruling over and abiding in this peaceful state of the soul by his Divine wisdom; or, in other words, by Melchizedek, the king of righteousness and of peace, is meant that peaceful and comforting influence of the Spirit of Truth as felt in the rational mind, that calm reliance, that firm and abiding faith in the Divine Truth, that clear perception of the goodness and beauty of the religious life. And by Melchizedek the Priest is meant the presence of the Lord in the mind as the dispenser of all heavenly love and goodness. For the Priest is the representative of the Lord as to the Divine goodness and mercy, while the King represents Him as to the Divine wisdom and justice. And, finally, by Melchizedek bringing forth bread and wine we have pictured to us

7*

the actual nourishment which our souls, in those states of internal peace, receive chiefly from the Lord, as the Giver of all goodness and truth, of all charity and faith, thus of our spiritual bread and wine.

Bread and wine are the natural elements corresponding to the two kinds of nourishment essential to the soul. The soul actually lives upon love and truth, or goodness and wisdom, in some of their various forms ; it lives upon these as derived from some source without itself,—from God, their only Giver. The soul does not live of itself any morethan the body has its nourishment in itself.

By the Priest and King bringing forth bread and wine is clearly figured forth, therefore, the Lord as the Giver of all goodness and truth, feeding the human soul with these the elements of spiritual and immortal life. It is in the same sense that the Lord is called the Bread of life, the Bread of heaven, and also the Vine, and his Blood the cup.

It is in this sense that even to-day the Lord our Saviour comes forth here at the gate of peace, our true Melchizedek, our everlasting Priest and King, and offers us the Bread of heaven and the Cup of salvation.

It is his own Blood that He offers us as the wine of the soul, his own Body as the bread of eternal life. Because the Lord's glorious Divine Body is itself, in its primary and very substance, the essential Love and Wisdom from which are the life, substance, form, and existence of all created things in heaven and on earth.

This life-giving, soul-refreshing substance the Lord offers us for our actual appropriation, for our voluntary acceptance here amid the warfare and toil of our earthly bodily life. He condescends to come down into the plane of visible, tangible substance to offer these his Divine gifts under the form of earthly bread and wine, and Himself, the true Priest, to be represented by those his human servants who

minister at the altar of his Church on earth.
In this way, in the Sacrament of his own ap-
pointment, He would declare to our natural
senses, if necessary, the great truth that He
alone is the Source of all Life and Blessing,
and He would enable us, by actual partici-
pation in this Holy Supper, to show forth in an
equally real, visible manner our faith in Him
as our Redeemer, our reliance upon Him as
our Father, our remembrance of Him as our
Saviour, our love for Him as our Priest, and
our obedience to Him as our King.   For when
as the eternal Priest He had instituted his Holy
Supper, then as our everlasting King He commanded us, saying, "This do in remembrance
of me."

Let Christians, then, thankfully and with rev-
erent hearts receive this spiritual bread and
wine offered them under the form of a Sacrament by the true Jerusalem's Lord and King.
It may be that we, too, come from the midst
of conflict, our hearts soiled by too close com-

mingling with the world, our spiritual energies faint and weary after long struggle against our besetting sins; or, perhaps, slow and sluggish from long indifference and careless yielding to the evil.

In any case, let us come with sober, thoughtful minds, carefully searching our hearts and secretly confessing our unworthiness to God. We must put the shoes from off our feet, for the place we are about to enter is a holy place. We must leave aside the cares of the world, and all earthly affections and thoughts. We must banish all warring anxieties from our minds and approach in heart the heavenly Salem, the city of peace. There thankfully and gladly let us wait upon the Lord; confident that through the outward form of the Sacrament will be communicated to us that inward, invisible, but real grace which is the Bread and Wine of the soul, and in receiving which we are truly blessed in the name of the Lord.

D*

V

Abraham and Sarah in the Land of Abimelech; or, the Divine Adaptations of Truth to Men.

And Abimelech took sheep, and oxen, and menservants, and womenservants, and gave them unto Abraham, and restored him Sarah his wife.—Gen. xx. 14.

THAT the Bible is man's only guide to faith and to salvation is a doctrine generally acknowledged among Christians. With too many professing to be Christians the whole matter ends with this acknowledgment; neither faith nor salvation being with them concerns of such weighty and practical importance as to induce them often to resort to the only guide, however unquestioned its authority may be. Others, devout and earnest readers of the Divine Book, while entertaining a general belief in its sanctity and plenary inspiration, yet find in their own experience that it is only certain portions that

82

really afford them much direct information on
spiritual subjects, and that even this much is
of a nature quite different from the kind of
instruction considered necessary in other de-
partments of knowledge. It neither resembles
the transcendental theories of the philosophers
nor the angular and matter-of-fact dogmas of
the theologian ; and the benefit derived from
perusing this holy book of God's Truth is, accordingly, experienced by most of this class of
readers as being rather that which attends a
devout and humble state of mind in waiting on
the Lord than any definable amount of doctrinal information. These persons, too, believe,
and most rightly, that in having the merciful
providence of God recalled to their minds by
the histories of his wonderful dealings with
his chosen people of old, and by the far more
touching and eloquent record of his own
blessed life on our earth and of the glorious redemption wrought for all the children of men,
the soul of the Christian is encouraged in its

reliance upon the Divine mercy and in its hope
for final deliverance from evil.   Now, this outside view of the Holy Word is not to be regarded as a trivial one or as without its own
degree of usefulness.   The truth is, that far
more depends upon the state of mind in which
one comes to that Divine Fountain of Living
Waters, than the amount of knowledge concerning its great depths of truth which one
has, for the time being, stored safely up in
the intellect.   *The hungry are filled with good
things, and the rich are sent empty away.*

The sacred narrative relates how Abraham
once journeyed southward with his wife Sarah
until they came to Gerar.   Arriving and so-
journing here, Abraham fears that the men
of that land desiring his wife, who was a
woman fair to look upon, would slay him, her
husband ; and, accordingly, he instructs Sarah
to pass for his sister, and not his wife.   Now,
Abimelech, hearing that Sarah is the sister of
Abraham, sends for her, meaning to take her

to wife; but the Lord warns him in a dream in the night that Sarah is already Abraham's wife, and commands that she be restored to her husband. Abimelech, rising up early in the morning, expostulates with Abraham, and asks him why he allowed Sarah to go for his sister when she was his wife; Abraham replies that he thought, "Surely the fear of God is not in this place; and they will slay me for my wife;" and, therefore, he begged his wife to say of him, into whatever place they should come, "He is my brother." Now, this was, indeed, true; for Sarah was the daughter of Abraham's father, but not of his mother. And then follow these words, "And Abimelech took sheep, and oxen, and menservants, and womenservants, and gave them unto Abraham, and restored him Sarah his wife."

Read in the sense of the letter, as the Christian Church has hitherto alone been able to read this narrative, it appears in every way remarkable. As a guide to our conduct,

we would in nowise be justified in adopting it.
As an instance of God's wise providence, it is,
in its many literal aspects, utterly beyond our
comprehension. Yet this is surely a part of
that Word of God which alone can make us
wise unto salvation.   Just as much a part, just
as essentially the Divine Word, the heaven-
sent lamp to our feet, as the Lord's Sermon
on the Mount, or the Parables of the Kingdom
of Heaven. And when the diligent reader
finds that the remarkable conduct displayed in
this narrative is presented to us not once only,
but three times in God's Word ; that Abraham
when he sojourned in Egypt likewise published
that Sarah was his sister and allured Pharaoh
to take her from him, and that Isaac in the
land of Abimelech did also suffer his wife Rebecca to be regarded as his sister,—when
these three similar instances of such remarkable conduct are thus distinctly set before us,
how can we account for the fact except on
the hypothesis that there is a deeper signifi-

cance contained therein than appears in the
mere literal account; that there is a spirit
within which truly "maketh alive" this dead
letter of historical narrative? What a marvelous and at the same time most satisfying truth
is that, then, which teaches us that one of the
sublimest and holiest, and at the same time
most practical, doctrines of Christianity is here,
under the veil of history, presented to our
minds! Who can but wonder, and feel as one
dazzled by the break of day upon a world of
darkness, when he learns that in this narrative
is minutely described a passage of the inner history of our Saviour's life in the flesh? I say
"inner history," for it pictures that development
of his mind, that gradual changing of his spiritual nature by which He was casting off the
material and mortal and putting on the pa-
ternal and the Divine which was to glorify
Him fully with the Father's glory. These
things, deep and mysterious, in our Saviour's
history are nowhere told in the *letter* of the

Holy Word, whether in Gospel, in Psalm, in Moses, or the Prophets. But in the spiritual sense of all these books is recorded for our edification and our guidance to heaven all the marvelous history of our Lord's inner life while in the world.

Now, if we would read this narrative in its spiritual sense, we must know what is the significance of the persons and places mentioned therein. As regards the persons, Abraham represents the Lord Himself as the Divine Good and also the Divine Humanity; accordingly, both the essential Divinity and the humanity assumed by it for the purpose of Redemption. Sarah, as his *wife*, represents Divine Truth conjoined with Divine Good, made one with it in the Divine Life, which is the Divine Proceeding. Sarah, as Abraham's *sister*, represents rational truth, or truth entertained from the reason only, and accordingly not in its essence conjoined and made one with the life of love. Abimelech, the king of Gerar, represents one

receptive of the doctrine of faith; and Gerar,
or the land of the Philistines southward, signifies a state of intelligence in matters of faith
and doctrine. Abraham's journeying southward, then, and abiding in the land of the
Philistines, in Gerar, denotes the Lord in his
assumed humanity while receiving instruction
in spiritual doctrine, which instruction was
alone from the Divinity within Him.

Seeing now the spiritual significance of those
persons and places, let us read the narrative
anew, and observe what lesson in spiritual
matters is here imparted to us. Our Lord, we
thus learn, when He comes into the perception
of spiritual truth, and is storing his mind with
the doctrine of faith, although as the Divine
Father He knows that all truth must be of celestial origin, and can live only when ultimated in
charity; still, as the Son born into the world in
our nature, in order that his mind may be developed in truly human order, He first regards
truth merely as rational truth,—that is, as truth

that can be reasoned out, be constructed in man's own intelligence, and thus belong to the intellect as its own. While in the doctrines of faith, that is to say, in a believing, receptive state of mind, He as Abimelech sends for Sarah. But Sarah is no longer the wife, that is, truth married to goodness; but, on the contrary, she is regarded simply as the sister, as truth, to be rationally received in the mind, and there to remain unmarried to any good, and related to good only as a sister to a brother. And thus Sarah—rational truth—comes to and is received in his mind. But the truth of faith is not thus always held as mere rational truth in the Lord's mind. The Divinity within Him after a season warns Him that this truth properly belongs to charity, and should be united to charity as its lawful mate; that it is a crime and an offense against the heavenly law of marriage that Divine truth should be held apart in the mind as mere rational intelligence, and not united to the affections of the will, and thus

become one Divine and perfect life, fruitful in
the offspring of righteousness and good works.
The Lord, warned in this manner, as Abimelech is described as being warned in the night
in a dream, comes now into a state wherein He
clearly perceives that truth of faith is of celestial and not merely intellectual origin ; that it
really comes from the Divine Love, in its origin,
and must be restored to unity with it ; that
while it seemed, when first received, to be
merely the outgrowth of the human intellect,
and thus quite independent of the will, now
it proves to be verily Sarah, the married wife
of Abraham, or that celestial truth which exists
only in union with the Divine Love, and thus
alone brings forth the offspring of charity and
good works, Then the Lord, still as Abimelech
in the doctrine of faith, takes oxen, and sheep,
and menservants, and womenservants, and
gives them unto Abraham, and restores to
him Sarah his wife. Perceiving as He does,
through his Divine enlightenment, that all the

truths in his intellect come from the love of
God as their source, He willingly restores
them to their owner, regards them as one with
and inseparable from the life of charity, and,
together with this acknowledgment, He renders
up to this Supreme Love, to the control of this
marriage union of goodness and truth, all the
lower and subservient qualities of his mind;
all his natural affections and natural thoughts,
all the goodness He possesses, all the truth He
possesses, whether natural or rational, He now
gratefully renders up to that Divine and Supreme Master, his own Divinity, the indwelling
Father, and thus from being human He becomes Divine, and by this process of his glorification He is made not only our Saviour in
time, but our great Pattern and Guide to all
eternity in the work of our regeneration.

A remarkable illustration occurs in this narrative of the correspondence, or signification,
of Scripture names. We have seen that Abraham represents the Lord when receiving in-

struction in spiritual doctrine. So far as He is
regarded as journeying into the southern land
and abiding there this is the case ; but when his
first rational reception of doctrinal truths is
referred to, the signification is at once trans-
ferred from Abraham to Abimelech. Abraham
then represents the Lord God in his celestial
degree, or as to the Divine Good ; Abimelech
the king represents the Lord first receiving
the truths in matters of doctrine as merely
rational, while He was on earth and his humanity not yet glorified. And so again Sarah,
as we have seen, represents, as the *wife* of
Abraham, the *Divine Truth* united to Divine
Love, or the spiritual and celestial natures of
God conjoined. As the *sister* of Abraham, in
which character she was sought by Abimelech
for his wife, Sarah represents *rational truth*,
which is addressed to the intellect only, and
not yet conjoined with any affection of the will.
We may now, too, gain some idea of the meaning of those other narratives which describe

the similar conduct of Abraham with his wife in Egypt, and of Isaac with his wife in this same land of Gerar. Why did Abraham twice deny his wife Sarah and allow her to be regarded as his sister, once in Egypt and once in Gerar? And why, again, is Isaac related to have once done the same? The answer to these questions is, in brief, thus: that our Lord, in assuming our human nature, underwent, as to his humanity, the same kind of mental and spiritual development that man undergoes; consequently, the various degrees of his mind were opened not all at once, but successively, and according to an eternally established Divine Order. Now, all the truth that the mind receives may be distinguished into various grades or kinds, and so, likewise, is the mind itself capable of a corresponding progressive development, each degree of the mind being fitted to the reception of its own degree of truth. These degrees we may call in their order, beginning at the lowest, the sensual, or scientific,

the rational, the spiritual, and the celestial.
Now, because this is the Divine order,—that
order into which man is created, and by which
he alone can become regenerated,—therefore,
when our Lord assumed our common humanity
that He might glorify it and make it Divine,
his own mind underwent this same gradual
and successive development. His being first
instructed in mere sensual knowledge, or
scientifics, is what is meant by Abraham's so-
journing in Egypt; and that He, who in his
indwelling Divinity was all Truth and all
Goodness Himself, might yet, in this assumed
humanity, enter into the experience of our
common boyhood and, as a boy, learn, with
avidity, and for the mere sake of learning,
without any regard to the uses of charity, the
knowledge of material science,—therefore is
Abraham said to deny his wife and to give
Sarah as his sister to Pharaoh, king of Egypt.
Thus is that universal law of Divine Providence
illustrated, that, although all truth, even in the

degree of sensuous or scientific knowledge, is
truly Divine, and exists *in its origin* in eternal
marriage with the Divine Love ; still, in order
that it may be adapted to our as yet unregenerate and natural minds, it takes for the time
the appearance of being merely sensual and
material, the demonstration of our five senses,
and neither Divine nor human, but simply
"matter of fact," as we say, and capable of
being learned by us regardless of any motive
of charity or use, and solely for our selfish
gratification.   So, after the law of his own
merciful providence, did our Saviour, when a
boy, refuse to learn sensuous truth as spiritual,
but rather made his humanity like ours by
learning the truths of science in the Egyptian
land, just as we must, from purely natural
ends, and receiving it in the natural, scientific
plane of the mind only.   Nevertheless, Pharaoh
did not take Sarah to wife, but restored her to
Abraham, no longer as his sister, but as his
married wife.   This teaches that our Lord,

when He had fully acquired his instruction in
scientific things, perceived, by intuition from
the Divinity within Himself, that the truth He
had learned was not given for its own sake,
but that it truly belonged, as a spouse, to the
love of use in the will, that to this love it should
be given up, and thus rendered fruitful and a
living good to all mankind; and also by this
recognition of Sarah as Abraham's wife is
implied the acknowledgment that all truth,
even the scientific, has its celestial origin in the
Divine Mind alone. But in the narrative which
we are to-day considering, the Lord is described
as being instructed in another higher kind of
truth. It is no longer in Egypt, but in the
land of the Philistines, that Abraham and Sarah
now sojourn. That the Divine Love and the
Divine Wisdom are now contemplated no
longer in things of science, but in the doctrinals of faith; for the land of the Philistines
represents those who are in those doctrinals;
and here again Sarah, or the spiritual Truth

of God, is not at first regarded as the wife of
Abraham,—that is, as the Divine Truth in conjunction with the Divine Love, and forming
one with it,—but rather as only the sister, as
mere rational truth, the outgrowth of the intelligence and the possession of the understanding alone, independent altogether of the heart.
But here, again, Abimelech is warned of God
in a dream, and gives up Sarah, restoring her
to Abraham as his wife; teaching us that the
Lord, in this stage of his education, after once
imbibing the truths of faith as mere rational
truths, then, by the intuition from the Divinity
within Him, comes into clear perception that
these truths also, the matters of spiritual
doctrine, of faith, and of religion, are only
barren and dead when entertained in the intellect as rationalities alone, and that in order
that they may bring forth the fruits of good
living, they must first be restored to their
marriage-union with the affections of the will,
and at the same time their celestial origin

acknowledged to be the very Divine Will itself.

In regard to Isaac, who, in the land of Abimelech, passed off his wife Rebecca as his sister, we are taught that he represents the Lord, not like Abraham as to his celestial nature, but as to his rational nature. Now, Isaac did not, like Abraham, go down into Egypt, and, consequently, only once presented his wife as his sister, and that in the land of the Philistines; and this means that the rational plane of the Lord's mind was kept above and distinct from the sensuous or scientific plane (represented by Egypt), and yet that this rational plane receives Divine Truth, first, only as rational, and that afterwards, by perception, it acknowledges that it is spiritual, that is, that it forms one with the Divine Love. In these three instances, then, we see the following progression of spiritual states: First, Pharaoh, in Egypt, takes Sarah as Abraham's sister, meaning to make her his wife; this is the natural desire in the youthful mind for sensuous or scientific knowledge, without regard to its celestial origin or its true use; by the wife restored to Abraham is meant the acknowledgment of the Divine Truth and of the holy use of charity in the plane of scientific learning. Secondly, Abimelech desires Sarah as the sister, not the wife, of Abraham, in the land of the Philistines. Here the spiritual man, in the doctrines of faith, desires rational truth, and accepts truth only as, or because it is, rational. But Abimelech also restores Sarah the wife to her husband, denoting that all the truths of faith, although received first as rationalities, must yet, in the end, be acknowledged to be Divine, and to belong only to charity in the will as their proper vivifier and counterpart. Finally, Abimelech, discovering Rebecca to be the wife, and not the sister, of Isaac, in the land of the Philistines, denotes that those in the doctrines of faith perceive ultimately that even in the rational plane of the mind rational truth is not sufficient of itself, but must be conjoined to rational goodness, and these both acknowledged to be Divine.

These are profound mysteries; so profound that it is almost in vain that we venture to explore them ever so slightly, for at most we can obtain but a glimpse into these vast expanses and fathomless depths of Divine wisdom which lie concealed beneath the letter of God's Holy Word. But we should take care not only lest we regard the entire narrative as in itself trivial and unprofitable, but also that when we learn of all these subtle distinctions and nice grades of meaning in the internal sense, we do not also look upon these with indifference and deem them too obscure and too profound for our daily wants in this mundane life.

Says Swedenborg regarding the important teachings contained in these and similar passages, "To the man whose interest and whose heart are engrossed in worldly and fleshly things these truths seem trivial. and as if conducive to no good whatever; but to the angels,

whose interest and affections are in celestial
and spiritual things, these truths are most
precious ; their ideas and perceptions of them
are ineffable.   Wherein it appears that many
things trivial to man because transcending his
intelligence are most highly esteemed by the
angels, because they enter into the light of
the angels' wisdom." (A. C. 2540.)   And now
if any one, acknowledging the profundity of
this narrative, is yet inclined in his own mind
to ask what is the practical lesson addressed, in
it, to us in the midst of our various worldly
pursuits and labors, I think the question may be
answered in a few words.   The lesson is this :
that in the natural and unregenerate state with
which we are born we are not capable of receiving any truth from the Lord at once as
spiritual or Divine truth; and if we were
capable of receiving it in its holy and celestial
character, while we remain the wicked beings
that we are, we should only be constantly pro-
faning and adulterating it, and thus closing our

minds against all heavenly and divine influences, and accordingly turning this precious
gift of God into the very instrument of our
spiritual ruin. This being the case, the Lord
mercifully provides that inasmuch as we cannot
learn truth in its real nature, we may learn it
under appearances adapted to our low states.
In youth, we learn the sensuous or scientific
truths, which, indeed, are only apparent and deceptive, but still are all the truths that we are
capable of receiving. We have to regard our
senses as the only reliable guides to knowledge:
we have to think of God as a King or Father,
ruling a kingdom, somewhere in space, and as
feeling kindly toward us when we do well, and
angry when we do wickedly ; we cannot yet
conceive of any real spiritual attributes, or of
spiritual existence ; consequently, our ideas of
God and of heaven are only sensuous ones,—
that is, formed after the nature of the knowledges obtained through our senses. Now,
supposing that these apparent truths were

taken away from the child and he had only to conceive of God as He really is in his spiritual nature and Divine infinity and perfection, what would become of the child's notion of God, and consequently of religion, of obedience, of heaven, and the life to come? And so, also, when we come to mature age and begin to look at things from the rational plane of our minds, then the truths of faith are presented first as rational truths; they are regarded, studied, received, or rejected, only as rational, or as addressed to the reason, and not to the will of man. As yet we have no perception of them as spiritual truths. This perception comes only from a life of obedience to the truths of doctrine after they have been intellectually received and approved. Supposing that no one of these holy truths of the Lord's own wisdom were implanted in our minds, or obtainable by our intellectual effort until we could perceive its Divine origin and nature, and could at once receive it with our affections and act it out in the life from a pure love of the truth itself, how many truths could we in our sinful earthly condition thus receive?

Therefore it is that God in his mercy provides that we may *learn truths before we love them*, that we may accept intellectually or rationally the doctrines of religion, and live in accordance with them, from simple motives of obedience, or for the sake of honor and gain, while yet we have little or no perception of their spiritual character and of the holy marriage which must exist between these truths and the affections of our wills before they can bring us into the heavenly life. Thus the Lord, as Abraham, allows the Divine Truth, which in Him exists only in heavenly marriage with the Divine Love, to appear to our minds not as Sarah the wife, but as Sarai the sister,— that is, not as the spiritual truth which it really is, but as the rational truth which it apparently is. But like Pharoah and like Abimelech, if we will not be utterly destroyed for the great

E*

crime of profanation of that which is holy and belongs to the Lord alone, we must, in due time, restore this truth to its celestial origin, in the ackowledgment of its spiritual and real nature; and holding all our sensual, all our rational knowledges and affections in obedience and in subjection to this truth, now perceived to be Divine, we must make it our living faith, by uniting with it all the purposes and motives of our life, and thus render it one with charity. Thus, like Abimelech, we shall have followed the Divine instruction; we shall have taken "sheep, and oxen, and menservants, and womenservants, and given them unto Abraham, and restored to him Sarah his wife." And then, too, offering up to our heavenly Father, the Giver of all goodness and truth, our whole hearts and minds in a life of devout and faithful obedience to his commands, we may say unto Him in grateful prayer, as said Abimelech unto Abraham, "Behold, my land is before thee: dwell where it pleaseth thee."

VI.

𝕳𝖆𝖌𝖆𝖗'𝖘 𝕽𝖊𝖙𝖚𝖗𝖓 𝖙𝖔 𝖍𝖊𝖗 𝕸𝖎𝖘𝖙𝖗𝖊𝖘𝖘; 𝖔𝖗, 𝖙𝖍𝖊 𝕾𝖚𝖇𝖒𝖎𝖘𝖘𝖎𝖔𝖓 𝖔𝖋 𝖙𝖍𝖊 𝕽𝖆𝖙𝖎𝖔𝖓𝖆𝖑.

And the angel of the Lord said unto her, Return to thy mistress, and submit thyself under her hands.—Gen. XVI. 9.

THE woman who talked with the Saviour by the well in Samaria, when she went thence, said to her acquaintance that she had seen a man who had told her all the things that ever she did, and asked, Is not this the Christ?

In like manner we come in our day to draw water from the deep well of Divine truth. We open the sacred volume which we call holy and regard as holy more from custom, perhaps, than from genuine appreciation of its character. We read a simple, ancient tale, savoring of a far-distant clime and of an age long past. In the literal story itself, majestic even to the

sublime as is its sad and touching style, there
is yet nothing that distinctly marks it as Divine,
or that conveys to the superficial reader any
spiritual lesson.   And yet if, searching its
interior depths, we should come upon a revelation of the things of our own heart; if we should
find here unfolded those secrets of our inner
experience which no human eye has ever
penetrated, no human ear heard uttered; if
within this Holy Scripture, beneath the natural
imagery of the letter, we should find a record
telling, indeed, of our spiritual or inward life,
all the things that ever we did, then, astonished
at this more than human wisdom and insight
into the heart of man, shall we not say, with the
Samaritan woman, Come and see! is not this
the Christ?   Shall we not behold, in the wondrous truth revealed out of the depths of the
sacred Scriptures, that Word which, in the Beginning, was with God and was God,—that
Word, indeed, which, now being unfolded to
man in its interior and its spiritual meaning, is

none other than the Christ, the Messiah which
was for to come?

It goes for little, in this our day of daring
speculation and unreined denial and dispute,
to declare to men that the Bible is indeed true,
and the very Word of God; that it is the connecting link between the minds of all rational
beings in the natural and spiritual worlds; that it
contains three senses,—the natural, or earthly,
which is the sense of the letter; the inner, or
spiritual, which treats of spiritual substances,
experiences, and states; and, lastly, a celestial,
or inmost sense, treating of the Lord, and the
purest essence or end of being. One word of
doubt or denial from the external sensuous
reason of man is more powerful than all the
arguments which can be brought to him on the
plane in which he reasons. So no mere rumor
or announcement of the Divinity of Christ
affected the belief of either Jew or Samaritan
regarding Him. The Samaritan woman doubt-
less mistook her Redeemer for a common way-

farer. The secret He told her out of her own
life declared to her his Divine omniscience; and
she went away, asking, Is not this the Christ?
And when men at this day, even they who
treat the sacred volume familiarly, with the air
of truth-seekers at life's wayside, examining
with a kind of condescension this wayfaring
Son of man, when they are told the thing which
no human voice could speak, no discrimination
of human friend, or foe, could pry out of the
secret depths of the actual experience of life,
then may these do well to pause reverently in
this mysterious presence, to remember that it
is alone the Messiah which is to come, which is
called Christ, who will thus tell us all things;
and not a few have felt the Divine voice saying, by a powerful intuition, which they cannot
resist, "I that speak unto thee am He."

It is, indeed, true that the whole Bible tells
in its inner sense the experiences of the human
soul. But there are few passages that appeal
so directly to the mind of so-called rationalistic

or free-thinking men as does this same strik-
ingly beautiful figure presented in the story of
Hagar. How little would the reader of the
mere letter imagine what a depth of the human
experience of our day lies concealed in this
picture of Hagar sitting by a fountain in the
wilderness, in the way to Shur!

Let us take a hasty glance at the literal
narrative itself.

Sarai, Abram's wife, has borne him no child.
She gives him her Egyptian handmaid, Hagar, to be his wife. But Hagar, when she
had conceived, despised her mistress; and
Sarai seeing that she is despised in the eyes
of the handmaid, sends Hagar away into the
wilderness. And there Hagar, sitting by a
fountain of waters, is comforted by the angel
of the Lord, who commands her to return to
her mistress and submit herself to her. He
promises that she shall bear a son, whose name
shall be Ishmael. And this one shall be a wild
man. His hand will be against every man,

and every man's hand against him. And
Hagar called that place the "Well of Him that
liveth and seeth me,"—" Beer-lahai-roi."

And now let us as hastily glance at the
spiritual meaning of these personages.

Abram signifies the internal man, or that
part of our human nature which draws its life
directly from the Divine source of all life, and
which is separated by a discreet degree from all
merely natural, bodily sense and thought. In
a good sense, therefore, Abram represents the
spiritual man as to his will or affection of
good; and Sarai the internal man as to faith or
affection of truth; especially does Sarai, as
contrasted with Hagar, represent that faith or
firm belief in spiritual and revealed truths
which comes from a love of such truths and
the good they teach; for this is the union with
Abram which Sarai his wife enjoys. Sarai,
the wife of Abram, is that truth which is ad-
joined to the goodness of this internal or spiritual man. She represents, therefore, spiritual

or intellectual truth as distinct from mere sensuous or scientific knowledge. And Hagar,
the Egyptian handmaid, represents the life of
the external or natural man, and its affections
for natural, materialistic science, or those kinds
of knowledge which we derive through the
senses from the external world. We have in
these three characters, therefore, a representa-
tion of the powers and agencies of every man's
mind. For every man's mind, or intellectual nature, possesses an internal, or spiritual part, and
external, or sensuous part; and between these
a third plane or degree, which partakes of both
the spiritual and sensuous and in a sense unites
them, and this is the rational faculty, or the
plane of the reason. And as we have seen
Abram and Sarai typify the spiritual plane of
the mind, in which reside the affections of good
and the truths of faith, Hagar, as a handmaid, represents the natural, or sensuous plane
of the mind, whose office is to serve the higher
faculties by the acquisition of scientific knowl-

10*

edge. She personifies the love of sciences
and knowledges. Egypt itself represents the
whole plane of scientific knowledge. That land
has always been regarded in secular history
as the mother of the physical and exact
sciences.

But what shall we say of the intermediate,
or rational plane of the mind? What is it
that typifies this? It is precisely to the origin
and office of the rational plane of the mind
that the narrative we are considering mainly
refers. For nothing else is treated of in the
internal sense of this passage in the story of
Hagar than the birth or formation in the mind
of the rational faculty. It is easy to see that
the reason stands midway between the mere
senses of the body and the knowledge they
acquire on the lower side, and, above, the perceptions or spiritual knowledges of the soul.
Now, all life, properly speaking, comes from
within. Life descends as love or affection from
the inmost chamber of our being, and inspires

and animates the lower planes of the mind, all our sensuous and bodily faculties and all the ideas or knowledges we take in from the outer world. It is by the union of the internal life, the spiritual principle of the internal man, with the bare and otherwise lifeless acquisitions of the outer mind, that there is formed what we call the reason. Mere knowledge, mere facts, stored up in the memory is not reason. But the love of knowledge and of acquiring scientific truths, which belongs to every man by nature, and which resides in the outermost part of the mind,—almost in the senses themselves,—this *love of knowing* must be infused with the higher and interior principles of the spiritual mind in order for a truly rational faculty to be produced. And this union between the life of the spiritual and that of the external, or scientific mind is what is typified by the union of Abram and Hagar, his Egyptian handmaid. From this union there proceeds that rational faculty, which is also typified by Ishmael, the son which Hagar bore to Abram.

We see now what elements of our common human nature are here placed before us as in an allegory, and personified by the various actors upon this stage of ancient and divinely constructed history. How eagerly and with what delight have men traced in the writing of a Shakspeare, a Dante, or a Bunyan, the underlying portrayal of our common human attributes and internal experience! But what shall we, in comparison, say of a sublime allegory like the one here presented to us in the story of Hagar and Ishmael,—an allegory which ceases to be allegory, and becomes veritably eternal reality and truth,—when we find that it is conceived by no mere human imagination, but by that wisdom of Him only who searcheth the heart and veins, from whom no secrets are hid, and to whom every thought and emotion of every human soul stands out in clear daylight, and is spoken as upon the house-top!

The first experience of the mind after acquiring the common facts pertaining to mere bodily existence, is the formation of the reason. The infant, the child, does not reason, but acts like the animal, from instinct. Gradually with the increase of knowledge there develops this higher faculty in which man is, as it were, to become master of his knowledge and of all his faculties ; thus to be no longer impelled by mere animal impulse or automatic instinct, but to choose, determine, and act from his own free judgment. It is evident that man's freedom consists in this, his having a reason whereby he may form his own conclusions and judgments. The brute has no freedom really, because it is impelled only by an instinct implanted in its nature. Man having freedom, can yield to or resist these similar animal impulses at his pleasure or will. And when the child grows to the years of discretion, or mature reason, then we call him free, and no longer a child, but a man. We see here the wisdom of the Creator, in that He has provided for the birth and growth of the rational faculty in man as the essential condition to all progress and happiness. But there is not a single gift of God to man which man may not, if he will, pervert and apply to improper ends. It is so with this sublime, this noble gift of reason. And since the *will* of man is what gives direction to all his conduct and what determines the use he will make of all his faculties, and since the will is, in our present condition, selfish, earthly, and inclined to sin, therefore the reason has become enslaved with the rest of the faculties, and instead of being the bold, courageous torch-bearer, leading us up to higher light and liberty, it plays the cowardly part of excusing our fleshly weaknesses and endeavoring to glorify the miserable creatures of our depravity and our spiritual blindness. The reason was given us to be indeed the step from earthly to spiritual science, to be the fruit of the marriage between Abram and Hagar, between the soul and the bodily sense. But, alas! the inner affection of the will which gives the reason its life is no longer pure and heavenly. It is fallen and corrupt. It is the father of lies, and the reason languishes under its tyranny. There is but one deliverance possible, and this does not lie in the mere facts of earthly science, the so-called "positive science," which men nowadays are so set upon acquiring. All this is dead and useless unless inspired by some higher, nobler end or motive of the heaven-born soul,—unless it becomes one with the faith and religion which makes up the life of the spiritual man. And for this all-enlivening, all-comprehending, all-reconciling spirit, this ransomer of our reason from the bonds of sensualism, this deliverer of our immortal souls from the grave of mere dead science, we must look to God, the Source of all Truth, and to his Revelation, and thus we shall know the Truth, and the Truth shall make us free.

So soon as Ishmael is conceived Hagar begins to despise her mistress. The first and natural impulse of the rational faculty on coming to consciousness in the mind is, to despise the things of faith and the facts of spiritual existence. The reason rejoices in independence, in absolute self-direction. Like the youth just entering upon manhood, it rejoices in its sense of freedom from all parental restraint; it is proud in its ability and its right to judge and determine for itself. Hagar despises her mistress Sarai. The age of the world we now live in would seem to be that of this newly-conceived, proud and defiant reason. The shackles of traditional faith, the tutelage of the past in things not of politics and physical science only, but in matters of religious faith as well, seem to have been thrown off. The human race would seem to be entering a new, vigorous stage of early manhood. Science and a love of science is now the chief object of its favor. Hagar, the Egyptian handmaid, is installed in the place of Sarai, the rightful mistress of the household. And Sarai is despised in her eyes. Not only are the things of traditional faith lightly esteemed by the popular opinion of our day, but spiritual motives and principles of any kind, yea, the existence of a spiritual or supernatural world, is regarded by many as only the fancy of dreamers and sentimentalists, and as things of little or no practical importance, whether real or not. The incipient reason released from the shackles of ignorance and superstition begins with despising the things of faith and religion. Happy is he in whom the reason, having thus begun, does not also end with this!

And what is the character of this Ishmael when born? "He will be," says the sacred text, "a wild man; his hand will be against every man, and every man's hand against him." How truly does this describe the newly born, unfettered reason of man! Its nature is to combat; to contest commonly accepted

theories; to deny, to argue, to dispute. Its
first attitude toward any truth it meets is hos-
tile, defiant.   It stands with a drawn sword
at the entrance of the mind to ward off mere
dogmatic or traditional assertions.   Its hand is
against every man's, and every man's hand is
regarded with suspicion, as if directed against
its own freedom.   It is as a wild man.

But it is of the Divine Providence that the
reason, when first developed in man, should
thus be left to its free and independent course.
It must learn by experience what is its true
use and position in the mind.   And if it reaps
desolation and unhappy, selfish solitude as the
reward of its universal doubting and deny-
ing of what others believe, and are happy in
believing, then will- it the more freely and
earnestly seek the protection and the guidance
of some higher authority, of some higher faculty
than itself.   This higher faculty is faith; the
higher authority is the spiritual truth residing
in the internal man.   It is Sarai, Hagar's

rightful mistress. And the voice of the Lord uttered in the still depths of the stricken conscience is that of the angel, saying to Hagar at the fountain, "Whither wilt thou go? Return to thy mistress, and submit thyself under her hands."

For the natural mind having rejected its faith in spiritual truth and despised it, will be found like Hagar, sitting at the fountain in the wilderness, in the way to Shur. Shur is a land bordering on Egypt, and the fountain of water is that kind of merely natural or scientific knowledge in which the mind of the unbeliever seeks to stay itself. But it is a fountain *in the wilderness* at best, and he who sits there is an afflicted one. Mere science without faith is as dead as the body of man without the soul; it is a universe without God; it may give meat and drink to mere bodily appetite, but leaves the immortal soul famishing for food.

O desolate and troubled soul! who hast rejected in scorn thy faith in God's Word and

Kingdom, and sought to live upon the poor crusts of merely earthly lore and riches, return to thy mistress, and submit thyself to her! Return to that faith which is the only light and enduring comfort of all that is truly human and immortal in thee! Think not that this is to sacrifice thy reason. It is alone what will make the reason free in the eternal truth, and make it the master rather than the mere slave of a corrupt and fallen will. For the voice that said to Hagar "Return," uttered also the sure promise that "Ishmael shall be born, and his seed shall multiply exceedingly." And for a perpetual memorial of this voice of the Spirit warning thee out of the still but awful depths of the Divine Word, call this place in thy life's history Beer-lahai-roi,—"The well of Him that liveth and seeth me."

VII.

Ishmael restored to Life; or, the Spiritual Reason.

*And God opened her eyes, and she saw a well of water;
and she went, and filled the bottle with water, and gave
the lad drink.*—Gen. xxi. 19.

THE story of Hagar and Ishmael is one
of those Divine allegories with which the
sacred Scripture abounds. It is remarkable
as being that one which the Apostle Paul especially designates as such, indicating at the
same time in a brief but grand outline something of the spiritual meaning underlying the
literal narrative. "For it is written, that Abraham had two sons, the one by a bondmaid,
the other by a freewoman. But he who was
of the bondwoman was born after the flesh;
but he of the freewoman was by promise.
Which things are an allegory: for these are

the two covenants; the one from the mount Sinai which gendereth to bondage, which is Agar. For this Agar is mount Sinai in Arabia, and answereth to Jerusalem which now is, and is in bondage with her children. But Jerusalem which is above is free, which is the mother of us all."—Gal. iv. 22–26.

Viewed in the light of the spiritual sense, we behold here certain persons acting out as in a drama what goes on in the mind of every religious man. Hagar is the type of the purely natural love of knowledge, or that affection for learning which is born with every one, and which shows itself among the first traits developed in early childhood. Ishmael, the son which Hagar bore to Abram, represents the reason; for this faculty is born of the union of the natural love of knowledge with the interior or spiritual life of the soul. Animals know a great many things as perfectly as men do, but their knowledge remains only knowledge; it does not become reason, as it is itself never the result of any analytical thought, and this because it is not united with any spiritual desire or purpose. Man has two natures, or two planes of the mind, in which he receives life from God, and is conscious of it as his own life. The higher plane is the spiritual, the lower the natural. Thus he lives two lives,—one in the spiritual world, the other in the natural world. In his spiritual mind he is aware of spiritual things,—such as the truth of revelation; for instance, he knows and thinks about God, about his duty, about the life after death, about heaven and hell; in his natural mind he is aware of natural earthly things,—thus, his bodily wants, earthly riches and comforts, and the various occupations and sciences which relate to getting these things. Now when the knowledges of the spirit and the knowledges of the senses are united they give birth to another, middle plane of the mind, which is the rational. Here resides the reason,—midway, we may say, between soul and body, between religious faith and natural science. The reason is intended to unite the two, or is rather the effect of these being united. Through the reason the light of religion, of our spiritual nature,—thus, of faith and of conscience,—may come down into the acts and motives of our bodily life.

We have seen that when Ishmael is first conceived then Hagar his mother despises Sarai, Abram's true wife and her own rightful mistress. Sarai is faith, or the spiritual truth, and by her being despised by her handmaid Hagar is represented the light esteem, yea, the contempt, in which the things of faith are held when the reason, typified by Ishmael, is first being developed. And Ishmael, too, is a wild man, whose hand is against every man; which description applies equally to this reason, which brings to the mind a sense of independence and self-reliance, and a disposition to combat, to deny, to argue about whatever is presented as an object of belief. We have seen, too, in tracing the story of Hagar and Ishmael, how at a fountain of water in the wilderness the angel of the Lord appears to Hagar and warns her to return to her mistress, and submit herself under her hands. And in this event we have seen typified the mind of man which has relied on its own reason and has sought to look to natural science alone for all truth, now warned by the Spirit of God to return to its rejected faith, and to seek in the doctrines of revealed religion those truths which alone can have authority in the soul and can bring it any enduring refreshment and comfort.

But let us pursue this wonderful narrative with a view to further instruction, contained in its spiritual meaning, concerning the place and office of the reason in relation to faith.

Ishmael is born, and Hagar returns with this her son to the house of Sarai her mistress. But after a time Sarai also bears to Abram a son, whose name is called Isaac. And we

F*

read that Sarah saw the son of Hagar the
Egyptian, which she had borne unto Abraham,
mocking; and she said unto Abraham, "Cast
out this bondwoman and her son: for the son
of this bondwoman shall not be heir with
my son, even with Isaac. And the thing was
very grievous in Abraham's sight because of
his son. And God said unto Abraham, Let it
not be grievous in thy sight because of the lad,
and because of thy bondwoman; in all that
Sarah hath said unto thee, hearken unto her
voice; for in Isaac shall thy seed be called.
And also of the son of the bondwoman
will I make a nation, because he is thy seed.
And Abraham rose up early in the morning,
and took bread, and a bottle of water, and
gave it unto Hagar, putting it on her shoulder,
and the child, and sent her away: and she
departed, and wandered in the wilderness of
Beer-sheba. And the water was spent in the
bottle, and she cast the child under one of the
shrubs. And she went, and sat her down over

against him a good way off, as it were a bow-shot: for she said, Let me not see the death of the child. And she sat over against him, and lift up her voice, and wept. And God heard the voice of the lad; and the angel of God called to Hagar out of heaven, and said unto her, What aileth thee, Hagar? fear not; for God hath heard the voice of the lad where he is. Arise, lift up the lad, and hold him in thine hand; for I will make him a great nation. And God opened her eyes, and she saw a well of water; and she went, and filled the bottle with water, and gave the lad drink. And God was with the lad; and he grew, and dwelt in the wilderness, and became an archer."

Out of this beautiful narrative, as from a casket of rare jewels, we would venture to pluck but one gem from its infinite store of heavenly truths. And this is the truth herein contained concerning the regeneration of man as to his rational mind, or in other words, his advance from natural to spiritual reason;

which is none other, when rightly understood, than the progress from the natural bondage under the law, which the apostle discerned, or the mere external recognition of the Divine commandments as to be obeyed through violent self-compulsion, to that higher willing service of the free spirit "whose delight is in the law of the Lord."

For man has one kind of reason before he is regenerate, and another kind after he is regenerate. The first may be called the natural reason, and the second the spiritual. For before a man has arrived at adult age and by a knowledge of his evils as sins, and by resisting temptation, he has begun to be actually a religious man, he has a reason, it is true, but a reason which regards nature as first and uppermost, and spiritual things only as in the second place. This natural reason admits the truths of the Bible, and the authority of the Divine law, and the religious doctrine, which have been taught by one's parents; but it receives them at the bidding of another, and on outward evidence, and not yet from that interior conviction which comes from having tested in real life and proved what these things really mean and are. This natural reason abides, therefore, in apparent rather than in real truths; it sees things in the deceptive, often false, lights of nature and the bodily senses. But so far as it does not deny these truths of doctrine, even its gross natural conception of them is useful, as affording a basis for that higher and truer knowledge which will come by the spiritual trials to be endured as one advances in years.

The first thing to be observed in this narrative is the fact of Ishmael's mocking at the birth of Isaac. For Isaac represents the higher reason, which is distinct from that born of man's external sensuous knowledge.* And

* In the Lord Himself, that Divine rational which from the indwelling Father replaced the merely human rational

there is at first a discordance and want of sympathy between this reason of faith, as we may call it, and the reason of the senses. Ishmael representing still the unregenerate natural reason, is true to his defiant, skeptical, negative character. *He mocks at Isaac,* even as Hagar his mother once despised her mistress Sarai. The same antagonism is here represented, between that sort of knowledge and the reasoning based thereon which comes in from our contact with, and study of, the natural world about us, and that other sort of knowledge and its reasoning which comes directly from heaven by revelation through the Divine Word and the doctrines of the Church thence derived; or which springs from a certain intuitive perception of the truth which accompanies a life of actual goodness. This mockery of Isaac by Ishmael is like the senses of the body

---

derived through the body born of Mary, is what is signified by Isaac.

mocking the mind because it believes in a world which it cannot see, and because it says that the body does not live of itself but only from the invisible spirit within. Or it is like our selfish and carnal appetites, which seek to get and to enjoy the utmost present gratification, and our ambition to acquire riches and distinction by whatever means will not outwardly disgrace us, mocking at those silent warnings of the conscience which speak of those evils which are sins, which tell us of God, of our higher obligations to Him, of our spiritual peril, and the awful future that awaits the willful transgression of the Divine commandments. Such is the mockery with which Ishmael, or the natural reason, saluted Isaac, which is the reason of faith.

Probably there are few persons who have made any experience in the religious life who have not at times felt very distinctly this antagonism between the reason of the spirit and that of the senses; or, as we would rather say,

the reason of the regenerated and that of the
unregenerated mind. Often in our own consciousness we are aware of the two opposite
modes of thought existing almost simulta-
neously. We see in a certain clear light, as
from the spiritual world, the great truths of
our faith; we have a clear conception of God;
we hold the Bible to be his Divinely-inspired
Word; we believe in the existence, close
around us, of the spiritual world, and in the
guardianship of angels, and the temptations of
evil spirits; we believe in the judgment we
must undergo after death, and in the eternal
life of heaven which awaits us if we have faithfully borne our cross in this life to the putting
away of our evils as sins against God. But
at the same time a voice out of this material
realm of nature seems to cry out in mockery,
"What do you know of all this? Have you
ever seen or touched or tasted any of these
spiritual things? How do you know that of
which the senses give you no knowledge?

What is the Bible but a history like any other? and what are religion and the doctrines of faith but certain inventions of the human mind, which are transmitted from one generation to another, and which, like civil laws and institutions, are preserved for the sake of the good order they promote, and their rules observed because custom or respectability requires it?" If we had to resort to external evidence—to the evidence of our senses—to prove that there is a God, a Divine law of life, a revealed Word of God, and a future life in a spiritual world inhabited by spiritual beings, we surely would find it difficult to bring satisfactory proof to the merely natural reason. Consequently, whatever we know of these spiritual things we know by a higher kind of sense, and by the convictions of a higher kind of reason. We know the things of faith not by ocular demonstration, not by handling and seeing, but by a direct light poured in from heaven upon the soul, enabling us to believe the things which we have learned, and in *light to see light.* Those receive this light who are already in the endeavor to bring forth that which they know of the truth in a holy and useful life. With these the reason itself becomes enlightened from heaven, and thus earthly and spiritual knowledge become conjoined and harmonized in the mind, and religion is no longer mocked by science, but reverently and lovingly served by her, and made in many ways more delightful and more beautiful and more powerful by this gladly-rendered service of her earthly handmaid.

But to return to the narrative once more. Ishmael and Hagar are sent forth again into the wilderness, and then, when on the point of perishing, the water in the bottle being spent, and Hagar having removed herself from her child in order that she may not see him die, again the angel of the Lord comforts her; he directs her to a well of water, and she, filling the bottle, gives the lad to drink.

And Ishmael grows up in the wilderness, and

God is with him ; and he becomes an archer. Now, we cannot fail to remark that the Divine Providence seems to be specially extended over Hagar and Ishmael. For this is the second time that in their desolation they have been comforted by the angel of the Lord. This evidently typifies that protection and preservation which the Lord provides for even the natural reason of man, and for this, too, when it is in enmity to spiritual truth, and in discordance with the faith entertained in the soul. The purpose of the mercy of God is not to destroy our reason as a bad and mischievous agent in the mind, but to elevate it into spiritual light, so that with a clear and justly-discerning eye it may look up and behold the things that are in heaven, or the world of spiritual knowledge, as well as to look down and see the things of the earth and material science.

But for the reason thus to be reconciled with faith, or, which is the same thing, for it to be receptive of any spiritual light, man must will-

ingly and deliberately renounce his self-depend-
ence and look up to the Lord, who alone gives
spiritual truth to the mind and gives faith to
the soul.   And yet so proud, so self-reliant, so
confident of its own sufficiency is the natural
reason of man, that it is only through periods
of bitter trial and desolation, through seasons
of doubt and the apparent destitution of all
truth, that man is brought to a sense of his own
helplessness and blindness, and of his need of
a Divine light and guidance.   Many, indeed,
there are whose souls are too weak to withstand the desolation of these dark and hungry
wanderings in the wilderness.   The Lord pro-
tects all souls from temptations greater than
they can bear.   Those who know nothing of
these trials of soul remain still on that level of
mere natural reason, accepting appearances for
truth, and abiding by the statements and the
authority of others.   But to prove the reality
of the spiritual reason, and know what is the
confidence of a spiritual faith, these are fruits

which can be earned only by the bitter lessons
of temptation and desolation.

These minds must be strong enough to
withstand long days and seasons of famishing
for truth, to feel the little spiritual strength,
with which they prided themselves, as belonging to their own selfhood, vanishing away like
the water and the bread which failed Hagar
and her child in the wilderness. And as Hagar
hid her child Ishmael under a shrub, and sitting
down a good way off, lest she should see him
dying, lifted up her voice and wept, so must
these souls have strength to see passing away
all that was most dearly prized, all earthly comforts and delights, it may be, but more surely
all those spiritual riches and merits in which
they had prided themselves; and chiefly must
they witness the utter abnegation and rejection
of all that merely natural reason which would
oppose itself to spiritual truth and would defy
its authority.

When the mind is thus cleansed of its delu-

sions and stripped of its pride, and, feeling its
destitution, actually thirsts for the refreshing
waters of Divine truth, then the Holy Spirit
descends into the soul, bringing with itself its
own peace, light, and comfort.   Guided by this
inward monitor, the humbled and chastened
soul turns to the spiritual truths revealed from
God out of heaven in his Holy Word, and finds
therein that wherewith to revive and strengthen
and refresh the whole man.   So "God opened
the eyes of Hagar, and she saw a well of water;
and she went, and filled the bottle with water,
and gave the lad drink."   Led thus from reliance on our own human prudence to put our
main trust in the providence of God, and from
the uncertain guidance of our self-will and its
cunning persuasions to the sure and constant
lamp of the Divine Word, our whole mind is set
right, and we are prepared with firm foot and
courageous heart to enter upon the conflicts
and the toils of our heavenward pilgrimage.
And Ishmael, who grows strong in the pres-

ence of God, shall become our archer.   That
enlightened spiritual reason which God now
gives to the soul, armed with the truths of our
holy faith and mighty in their Divine strength,
shall be our defender against all assaults of
falsity and unbelief.   Of him it shall be said as
of the Divine Prototype, "Thine arrows are
sharp in the heart of the king's enemies; whereby the people fall under thee."

VIII.

The Eternal Lamp; or, How Faith is to be Preserved.

---

*And thou shalt command the children of Israel, that they
bring thee pure oil olive beaten for the light, to cause
the lamp to burn always. In the tabernacle of the con-
gregation without the vail, which is before the testimony,
Aaron and his sons shall order it from evening to morning before the Lord.*—Ex. xxvii. 20.

THIS is the ordinance of the eternal lamp.
In the Tabernacle of the true Israel the
Lord commands that a lamp, fed with pure oil,
be kept forever burning before the vail of the
Testimony. From evening to morning it shall
ever be fed and trimmed, and kept burning
before the Lord.

The pattern of the Tabernacle was seen in
heaven. The Tabernacle is itself an image or
a picture of heaven, built upon earth, erected

144

by men's hands, and dwelt in by men ; it represents also the life of heaven brought down to
the life of this world. It is the true picture of
the Lord's Church upon earth ; for the true
Church on earth is a reflection of heaven, of
its order, and beauty, and glory, in the life of
men upon earth.

All those affections, thoughts, and states of
our life which make up in us the life of the
Church, or of heaven, are completely and un-
erringly portrayed by the Divine hand in the
descriptions of the Tabernacle furnished us in
the Bible. This carefully detailed account of
the Tabernacle is preserved to us after so many
centuries to this end, that it may ever speak to
us of the heavenly life, and guide us continually
toward that eternal House of God, not made
with hands, but prepared for our abode by our
Father in heaven. This Tabernacle of which
we read so much in the book of Exodus is,
like all the rest, a symbol of those unseen
and interior things of our actual life concern-

ing which the Divine Word is intended to instruct us.   It is not the mere structure itself
that is of spiritual interest to us, but rather
the meaning of it all ; and this is not difficult for
those to arrive at who look for a Divine meaning and cause in not only the outward and
visible things of God's creation, but equally in
his written Word.   Words are useful to us
only as we get at their meaning,—that is,
when we get at the mind that is in them.   So
a picture is not of value to us as so much
crude matter, but as representing something
which the mind sees and enjoys.   The Tabernacle of the Jews, were it now to be rebuilt,
would neither be a heaven or a church ; and,
therefore, as we build it in our imagination
while reading about it, we should remember
that the real heaven and the real church here
described is something which belongs to the
mind, and to the states and conditions of our
spiritual life.

The Tabernacle is the Church of the Lord

upon earth. In the inmost part of the Tabernacle was the Sanctuary, or the Holy of Holies.
Here was the Word of God, called the Testimony and the Covenant. It was kept in a
sacred depository called the Ark of the Covenant; and over it were the golden Cherubim,
which represented the protecting mercy and
providence of God. Before this Holy of
Holies hung a vail, and without the vail
were the place and the utensils of worship.
There stood the altar of incense, the table of
shewbread, and the golden lamp or candlestick. This was called the holy place. It was
in this holy place, outside of the vail of the
Testimony, that the perpetual lamp was ordained.

Now, when we think of the Church, not as
a building of wood or stone, but as a state of
truth and of life,—for the real Church consists
in this,—we shall not have much difficulty in
reading the spiritual meaning of this account
of the Tabernacle. The Holy of Holies is

where the Lord dwells most interiorly, secretly, and permanently with man. It is the highest, purest region of the soul; it is in the good and holy affections which the Lord inspires into man from Himself. It corresponds in the mind of man with the highest of the three heavens, or that heaven which is nearest the Lord. It is named the celestial heaven. The angels who dwell there are called the celestial angels, and love, which is the highest and most divine of all activities, is what most distinguishes their nature and life. The Lord dwells in the Holy of Holies when he dwells in the love or the pure affections of a man's soul. He dwells there not in a circumscribed personal sense, but even as He dwells in the Tent of Israel, namely, in the Ark of the Covenant and the Mercy-seat. For it is in the Covenant, Testimony, or written Word of God, that the Lord is approached, known, seen, and worshiped by man; and when this revealed Word, which is the Divine Truth itself, is hidden in the heart, is treasured in the soul's best affection, then is the mind verily a church or a tabernacle with its Holy of Holies, its place of the Lord's chosen abode. Then, too, may the Lord be approached and worshiped in his Mercy-Seat, or the Ark of the Covenant. For the man who believes and loves the Word of God, cannot but feel and know that there is constantly hovering over him an all-wise, all-loving Divine Providence, and in this perpetual providence of God he will feel that the Lord is ever dwelling near him, yea, in him, in the Mercy-seat.

But our best and purest affections are known to us only through our thoughts, and are proved and tested by our thoughts and our works. Although the Lord dwells most nearly and interiorly with man, in the abode of the affections, still is this to us all a secret abode. It is the secret place of the Most High: a place, like the Holy of Holies in the Tabernacle, into which none but the high-priest shall be per-

mitted to enter. And while we believe that
the Lord is interiorly present with all men, and
that He is especially conjoined with those who
know, love, and do the Word of His Covenant, yet is it not for us, with our finite and
human vision, to penetrate into the secret
modes of the Divine indwelling and operation
in the soul. There, within the vail, is the Ark
and the Mercy-seat. Within and beyond the
reach of our thought and knowledge is the
perpetual presence of the Lord within the
hearts of men, and the constant inflowing of
Life from Him. But without the vail we come
down to the plane of our conscious, thinking, reflecting, voluntary and seemingly independent life. Here is the place where we in
free deliberate choice bring our offerings and
bow down and worship before the Lord, who
is above all things in heaven and earth. Here
is where our affections must put on the shape
of thought and reason, and here is where the
perpetual lamp is to burn,—and that lamp is

the lamp of Faith. Here is the place where
our mortal steps may tread; the plane of our
free, spiritual agency, of our independent and
responsible human life as distinguished from
the Divine Life within, in which all alike live,
move, and have being. That should, indeed,
be a holy place. It should be furnished by
every believer in God with its altar of incense, its table of shewbread, and its ever-
burning lamp. From this, the plane of our
daily life before God, should go up daily the
incense of our prayer and worship. It should
present its offering of the good affections of
charity, its daily deeds of mutual love and
usefulness, and be ever illumined with the
light of a right and lively faith,—as with a
lamp of pure beaten oil to burn forever before
the Lord.

To derive more practical instruction from
this beautiful symbol of the Divine Word, let
us look more carefully to the purpose of this
lamp, and the way it is to be provided and

maintained. All these furnishings of the "holy place," the place before the vail, are indicative of worship offered up to the Lord. They are representatives of the acts of man's life, as these are accompanied by a recognition of the Lord and by obedience to Him; for worship consists in the regard a man has for the Lord in whatever he wishes, thinks, or does. Worship is not in the acts of life, but in the feeling and acknowledgment and purpose in which the acts are done. Now, this place called the holy place represents the spiritual mind; that is, a mind which is lighted up with the Divine Truth, which acts from faith in the truth, and which, consequently, is in a state of constant worship toward God.

The Lamp is the constant Faith of such a mind. It is only while such Faith in the Lord lasts that there can be any worship of Him; that there can be any good offerings brought before Him out of the fruits of life. The Lamp must burn constantly, day and night.

The Lamp ceasing to burn would be the extinction of Faith in the soul : it would be a man's ceasing to believe any more in God and in his revealed Word. The consequence of this would be not only mental darkness and universal uncertainty, doubt, and, at the approach of death, or of any earthly misfortune, despair and dread, but it would be also the end of all real goodness in a man's life. For his whole devotion, aspiration, and desire would now be thrown back upon himself, and self would become the idol now set up for worship, and the oracle to which he must resort for all natural and spiritual wisdom ; since if there be no absolute and revealed Divine Will and Wisdom, then is human will and its wisdom the highest to which we can look, and which, as a guide, we can follow. And let those who seek and follow this as the only true and safe guide, learn from short experience the extent of its ability to promote, unaided by Divine Truth, the good or the happiness of mankind.

G*

The man who lives not for God lives for himself;
and he lives not for God who does not believe in
God and seek to know God's will.   But to live
for God is to live believing in God, and ordering
our life, in every condition, calling, and act, by
the light of revealed Truth.   To live for God
is to have forever burning before the Holy of
Holies in our souls the Lamp of Faith fed with
the pure beaten oil of charity and good works.

And we have now to consider further these
three points: Who are to feed this Lamp?
With what shall it be fed?   And who are to
order it or keep it forever burning?

The people of Israel are commanded to
bring the oil for the Lamp.   This oil is to be
pure and of beaten olive.   And Aaron and his
sons, the priests, are to order and maintain it.

Aaron, the high-priest, and his sons represent primarily the Lord as the giver of all faith
and love.   But they also represent in a sec-
ondary and finite sense the ·ministry of the
Lord's Church on earth as that instrumentality

by which Divine truth, and thereby Divine
good, is administered to men.   It is the office
of the ministers of the Church to instruct the
people in the things of Faith, and thereby to
lead them to good of life.   They do not minister of their own, but of the Lord's truth, and
so far as they do this they, like Aaron of old,
represent the Lord, who is alone the Truth
itself.   In all the duties of their office the ministers by teaching the truth and leading men
to believe, love, and do it, do verily order and
keep burning the perpetual Lamp of Faith in
the holy place.   The preaching of the gospel,
the baptizing into the Divine name of Father,
Son, and Holy Spirit, the teaching to observe
all things commanded to the first Apostles
by our Lord upon earth, these duties are all
ordained for the one great purpose of im-
planting and cultivating in the minds of men
a true and living Faith in the Lord. The office
of Aaron is perpetuated in the true and everlasting Church of Jesus Christ.   The Lamp is

ordained for all generations, and it is now as
ever the duty of the ministry of the Church to
see that it be kept burning with a clear and
certain light from evening to morning,—that
is, through all the various states of life in the
minds of men.

But more than this, more than to keep the
Lamp lighted and in order, to keep the truth
which is given from above ever shining before
the minds of men, the priests cannot. It is
not the priests who are to bring the oil wherewith to feed this Lamp; and if the oil shall fail
the Lamp will go out. It is the children of
Israel who are to bring the oil. Faith, which
is the perpetual Lamp, cannot live without
charity, or the works of obedience and love,
any more than can a lamp burn without oil.
Oil is the good of charity in the daily life, and
it is only by living the truth, by bringing it
into the acts and relations of the every-day life,
that members of the Church really have Faith.
For Faith is not alive, it is not Faith, so long

as it consists in a mere knowledge of what is true, and a mere thinking of true precepts ; but Faith is the truth in us when it is obeyed and actually performed in the life we lead from day to day. It is plain that the priests can no more supply this actual goodness or charity of life wherewith to keep Faith alive in the Church than they can live and act as substitutes for the people. The priest can present the truth to a man's mind, but the man himself, with the Divine aid, does the rest. The priest may teach the truth given to him ; the man must bring it into actual life, must learn it, love it, obey it. Obedience to the truth in the acts of a good life, this is what both priest and people, as alike members of one Church, must furnish if Faith is to be preserved in the world, and if the Divine ordinance of the perpetual Lamp is to be obeyed by the generation of this day. Are there not too many, alas! who forget this ordinance requiring the children of Israel themselves to bring the oil for the Lamp, and who

think that the ministers are appointed not only
to keep the Lamp burning, but to furnish the
oil as well; not only to teach the truth of the
Church, but as substitutes for the people to
practice it, and so to keep Faith alive not
only for themselves but for others? It is a
fatal error to suppose that any man's Faith
is to be preserved by his minister; no priest
ever did or ever shall give to a man belief in
God or in religion. He can tell a man the
truth out of God's Word, but belief in this
truth must be acquired by the man himself
through a constant prayerful endeavor to
obey it in actual life. And this obedience to
the truth, this bringing it into contact with all
the motives, affections, and purposes of our
life in the world; this scrutinizing and dis-
criminating between good and evil; yea, this
crushing and grinding of our heart's purposes,
of our life's motives, under the hard rule of
absolute truth and duty,—this is what yields
that material with which we can alone keep

Faith alive; this is the pure *oil of the olive beaten for the light* which we, as children of the Lord's Israel, are to bring constantly to feed the eternal Lamp; with this, the rich fruit of our daily experience in endeavoring each one for himself to practice the holy doctrine which the Church teaches, with this, we are to keep forever burning and shining before the Lord a true, reasonable, and living Faith. The light of such a Lamp will make bright and beautiful the holy place before the vail of the Testimony. Fed with such oil, it shall never go out: evening and morning, in the hour of depression as in the hour of gladness and confidence, it shall burn bright before the Lord. In its light we shall come to the Holy of Holies with our worship, our prayers and thanksgiving, to our Father in heaven. Its shining shall ever point out to us, in the midst of the confusion, the doubts, the troubles and fears of this life, where is the Ark of God's Covenant and the Mercy-seat.

IX.

The Altar of Incense; or, the Faculty of Worshiping God.

And thou shalt make an altar to burn incense upon: of
shittim wood shalt thou make it. And Aaron shall burn
thereon sweet incense every morning: when he dresseth
the lamps, he shall burn incense upon it. And when Aaron
lighteth the lamps at even, he shall burn incense upon it,
a perpetual incense before the Lord throughout your gen-
erations.—Ex. xxx. 1, 7, 8.

AN altar of perpetual incense before the
Lord is here ordained for all generations
by the Divine Law. It forms a part of that
perfect order and form of the Church which
reflects its own image in the order and form
of heaven. As a literal, external ordinance,
the Altar of Incense is no longer obligatory,
because the Lord has now made known its
nature as a spiritual and internal ordinance.

As such, it is forever to be observed. Like every jot and tittle of the Divine Law delivered to Moses and ˜ recorded in the Old Testament, this ordinance of the Altar of Incense is still in force, in its true and spiritual, but no longer in its mere representative sense.

The Altar of Incense is a part of the furnishing of the Tabernacle, or Tent of the Children of Israel. The Tabernacle is the Church of the Lord; the Altar of Incense is a part of the actual life of every man in whom the Church is.

There is a spiritual meaning in the order in which the various parts of the Tabernacle are in the Divine Word ordained and described.

First in order is mentioned the Testimony, or the Law; this represents the Lord Himself. Then the Ark, or the inmost heaven, where the Lord dwells; then the table on which were the breads, by which are signified all good things of love which come from heaven; then the candlestick with the lamps, which represent

all the good things of faith; then is described
the Tent itself, or the Tabernacle, which is the
Church as constructed out of this love and
faith in the mind; thereupon is described the
altar of burnt-offerings, which represents the
regeneration of man as effected in the Church;
and last of all is mentioned the Altar of Incense; and this represents that which crowns
and completes the life and character of man
as a spiritual being, namely, the worship of
the Lord.

The worship of the Lord is what is spiritually meant by the Altar of Incense. The lifting or sending up to the Lord the faith and
the love which we have derived from Him,—
this is the spiritual ordinance of the perpetual
incense to be burned before the Lord in all
generations. Worship is all that proceeds
from love and faith with man, and is elevated
to the Lord. Man does not elevate anything
from himself to the Lord, but the Lord Himself elevates these things of faith and love to

Himself; and so lifts man up nearer to Himself, and more into the life of heaven. Worship itself is a faculty given us by the Lord: we can only worship the Lord from the Lord Himself dwelling in us. But this faculty of worship,—a faculty given to man during his efforts to be regenerated,—is one to which we should all give the most careful heed. It is because this faculty of worshiping God forms so essential a part of heavenly and eternal life that God commanded Aaron to make an Altar of Incense, and to burn incense thereon perpetually. There were, as we have seen, other things ordained in the Tabernacle, things which teach us the need of faith in the Lord, of the affections of goodness which He alone can give us to be the food of our souls, of the constant purifying of our hearts by the fires of temptation, and by the laver of the Divine Truth. But all these are insufficient to make our inner man an image of heaven and fit for eternal life in heaven if there be not erected

before the Holy of Holies in our hearts an
Altar of Incense, whereon morning and evening a sweet odor of true and sincere worship
shall be offered up to the Lord.

The faculty of worshiping God, so far as it
belongs to man's voluntary and seemingly independent life, consists briefly in this : in thinking of God, acknowledging and adoring Him.
All thought of God, and all love and acknowledgment and veneration of Him, come from
the faith and the love which God gives us from
Himself. But our own thoughts of God, accompanied by the acknowledgment of Him,
by reverence and obedience to Him, and hu-
miliation before Him,—these thoughts seem to
us to be voluntary on our part ; and these are
what make up, we may rightly say, the faculty
of worshiping God.

All true worship, like all true faith, must be
grounded in love to the Lord. By this we
mean, in a constant desire and effort to do the
Lord's commandments,—for our Lord says,

"He that hath my commandments, and keepeth them, he it is that loveth me." (*St. John* xiv. 21.) And this doing the commandments of the Lord is what constitutes the life of charity,— of doing what is right and good. But we can see how a man, having learned the Divine commandments, might, without acknowledging them to be Divine, obey them from selfish and worldly motives, in an outward manner, and be really worshiping the idol of self, and not loving God at all.

Therefore all good works, in order to be truly good, must be accompanied by faith in God,—that is, they must be done because God has required them, and the goodness that is in them must be seen to be the goodness of God and not of man.

Now, if love be the willingness to do what is right, and faith the teacher and guide in doing it, worship is that faculty whereby all the good works of faith and love are referred to the Lord as their only source, and whereby

alone we can do good unselfishly, and from that
love of goodness itself, which is love in the
Lord. While faith and charity are, therefore,
both, the necessary elements of all real worship,—since without faith we would have no
God to worship, and without love toward God
we would be wholly lovers and worshipers of
self,—yet, love and faith are incomplete without the worship of the Lord. In other words,
love or charity is not charity, nor is faith faith,
without the spirit of worship. For charity
without worship becomes mere self-righteous-
ness, or external morality; and faith without
worship becomes mere intellectual culture and
ability to do things that are right and seemingly holy from having learned them. But
the principle, or spirit of worship, is what
blends charity and faith into a holy, heavenly,
and truly blessed union. This inspires the
good deeds that are done and the holy truths
that are remembered with continual recognition of the Lord, and, therefore, makes these

continually receptive of new life from Him.
It is only when the good affections and true
thoughts of man are conjoined with their
source, the Lord, that they remain good and
true. Dissevered once from Him, they become turned into their opposites,—thus, into
what is selfish, evil, and false. Worship is that
connecting link that binds our souls to the
Lord; that keeps the golden chain of our
thoughts, motives, affections, and desires always suspended high up in the bright abyss
of heaven, enabling us to feel ever fresh impulses to do good, and to see ever brighter
and surer gleams of the light of truth.

We see, then, that while the essence and
life of worship consists in love toward God
and faith in Him, yet that it is a faculty distinct
from both loving and believing, and as a distinct faculty it must have its distinct exercise
in outward act. For worship, like love and
faith, must have not only its substance but its
form. There can be no love without some

exercise in good and loving deeds ; there can be
no faith without the learning and knowing of
some positive doctrines of truth ; so neither can
there be any worship, any lifting up of the things
of our heart and life toward God, without some
distinct, formal, conscious act of worship.   The
faculty of worshiping God can only be preserved and cultivated by actual exercise ; and
this exercise is performed whenever a man,
by a voluntary act of his mind,—accompanied,
it may be or may not be, by words of the
mouth and gesture of the body,—places himself
in God's presence and personally addresses
Him in the emotions of thankfulness, of adoration, of confession, of supplication, or of
praise.   In a word, worship is the intercourse
which a man seeks between himself *as a person*
and his Maker.   It is the expression in personal language and act of those general principles of charity and faith which should constantly find expression in the daily life.   Thus,
in doing the duty of one's calling, in laboring to

overcome temptations to sin, in remembering
the Word of God to do it, in all this there is as
a general principle both of love to God and of
faith, and in this there is the material, so to
speak, the unspoken soul of worship. But,
like thoughts which burn to be uttered on the
lips, like purposes which impel the body to
deeds, so this inward life of love and faith
seeks and demands its utterance in words. It
seeks its human, personal form, wherein it can
address its Divine Author in the language
of love, of praise, of confession, and prayer.
That such worship may be enjoyed by man,
and that this important need of our human
nature might be met, God has mercifully revealed Himself to us men, in Human Form,
and has enabled us to approach and worship
Him, in a Divine Humanity, as a known God,
as very God and Man ; and He says to all his
children, " Come unto me, all ye that labor and
are heavy laden, and I will give you rest."
" Cast your burden on the Lord, He will sustain

you." "Pray and faint not." "Ask and ye shall receive." "After this manner pray ye: 'Our Father, who art in the heavens, hallowed be thy name,'" and so on through the Divine prayer. Without the acts of external worship as outward formal expressions of our personal relations to God as a Divine Man, and as verily that Father in heaven on whom we actually depend for our daily bread as well as for all our spiritual life, we are in danger of losing, practically, all idea and sentiment of God as a Being to be worshiped; of ignoring all personal relations to Him, and of thus resolving Him, in our habits of thought, into a kind of abstract principle in nature, somewhat like the Deity of the pantheists or deists. Worship is the personal address of the soul to its known, revealed God, Saviour, Protector, Preserver, and Father in heaven. In the *Arcana Cœlestia*, *Num.* 10,177, we find this terse and striking definition of worship:

"When mention is made of worship, thereby

is meant *that holy principle* which is wrought by prayers, adorations, confessions, and the like, which proceed from the internal principles that are of love and charity." These things constitute the worship which is meant by burning of incense, as is manifest by the following passages. In the *Psalms*, we read, "My prayers are accepted: they are as incense before Thee." In the *Apocalypse*, v. 8, "The four animals and the four and twenty elders fell down before the Lamb, having each of them harps, and golden vials full of incense, which are the prayers of the saints." Again, "An angel having a golden censer : and there was given to him much incense, that he should offer it with the prayers of all the saints on the golden altar which is before the throne. The smoke of the incense ascended with the prayers of the saints." And in Malachi, "From the rising of the sun unto the going down thereof incense shall be offered unto my name, and a pure offering." i. 11.

Here let us carefully observe this definition of worship, which may be regarded as
authoritative doctrine. *First:* "It is a holy
principle" of our life and conduct; thus a
faculty and an experience distinct from all
others. *Second:* It is not natural or innate,
but rather comes by practice; for "it is
wrought by prayers, adorations, and confessions, and other like acts." And *Third:* It is
only wrought by these acts "when they proceed from an interior principle of love and
faith."

Love to God, or the Divine good which
flows into this love in our hearts, is the very
precious shittim wood itself of which the Altar
of Incense is built. The incense smoking on the
altar, sending up its fumes of delicious odor, is
the perfect symbol of the sincere worship of
man before the Lord. Man lights the incense
from the fire of his own desire to approach, to
adore, and supplicate the Lord. The fumes
rise of themselves; man does not lift them up.

So do the prayers of a sincere heart rise to God, because God draws them to Himself. For, as the great central Sun of all that is good and true, He attracts to Himself all the really holy and pure emotions of our hearts.

And, finally, the perfume of the burning incense is grateful to our senses, even as the sincere prayers and thanksgivings of our hearts are truly grateful to the Lord. The incense of spices signifies, we are taught, the grateful hearing and reception by the Lord of that which is elevated to Him out of genuine faith and love in the life of man. How beautiful, then, and how striking is this primeval symbol of the burning incense! The fumes rising from the altar are, indeed, like the thoughts and affections of a worshiping soul soaring above all mortal and earthly things into the pure, bright presence of God; and their sweet, clean odor tells of that Divine perception of the real quality of the worship

15*

offered up, and the Divine approval and joyful reception of all that is good and true therein.

Says the Psalmist, in the language which may worthily form a part of the Christian's ritual: "Let my Prayer be set for me before Thee as Incense, and the lifting up of my hands as the evening sacrifice." Our prayers and the uplifting of our hands are the elevation of our souls to the Lord; first, in the holy principles of life, and thence in the word and gestures of Divine worship. And not only in the evening, but both morning and evening was Aaron, the priest, ordered to burn incense on the Altar of Incense, before the Holy of Holies, the presence of God in the sanctuary. Well will it be for the Christian if, not only in a spiritual way, he offers up the worship of thought and affection to the Lord in all the varying states and experiences of life, but, especially, if he seek and strives earnestly, by the regular exercise of daily prayer, confession, and adoration before God, to cultivate that holy principle of worship which the Altar of Incense represents. For if we would realize that God is with us to protect and bless us, we must make real our personal relation, our approach and address to Him. If we forget that we are ever in the presence of Him, before whom all things in heaven and earth must bow down, then shall we forget that He is a God who is near to us, who cares for us, who will hear us when we call unto Him. Rather, by collecting the thoughts and coming reverently before Him, to lift the heart directly to Him in prayer and worship, let the Christian make it his daily habit to place himself spiritually in the holy place of the Tabernacle, there to burn a perpetual incense before God; yea, there, in the solemn but peaceful consciousness that "the Lord is in his holy Temple," to let all the earth keep silence before Him.

X

The Shepherd-boy made King; or, the Lord's Choice versus Man's Choice.

But the Lord said unto Samuel, Look not on his countenance, or on the height of his stature; because I have refused him: for the Lord seeth not as man seeth; for man looketh on the outward appearance, but the Lord looketh on the heart.—I. Sam. XVI. 7.

THUS was Samuel, the Lord's Prophet, instructed in making his choice of a king, that should be anointed to rule over Israel as the successor of Saul, who had disobeyed the Divine Word.

The Lord had sent Samuel to Jesse, the Bethlehemite, saying that He had provided a king from among his sons. And when Samuel had come to Jesse, he called him and his sons together to the sacrifice which he would make unto the Lord. And Jesse came, and seven of his sons with him ; but one son, the youngest, was left behind to tend the sheep. And Samuel looked on these sons of Jesse, one after another, to see which it should be that the Lord had chosen to be anointed king. And when he looked on the first, Eliab, he thought that the Lord's anointed was surely before him. We suppose he judged this from the face and imposing stature of Eliab. For when he so determined, the Lord at once addresses Samuel, saying, Regard not the face, nor the stature; for him have I rejected : the Lord seeth not as man seeth ; for man looketh on the outward appearance, but the Lord looketh on the heart.

And Samuel, being thus Divinely instructed, proceeded to view the other sons of Jesse as they passed before him one by one. But all seven passed by, and yet Samuel said, "The Lord hath not chosen these." And then, on inquiry, he learned that there remained yet

H*

the youngest son, who was tending the sheep. And Samuel said, "Send and fetch him: for we will not sit down till he come hither." And we read that Jesse "sent, and brought him in. Now he was ruddy, and withal of a beautiful countenance, and goodly to look to. And the Lord said, Arise, anoint him: for this is he. Then Samuel took the horn of oil, and anointed him in the midst of his brethren: and the Spirit of the Lord came upon David from that day forward."

Thus was David chosen by the Lord and anointed king over Israel. But it is not as a part of the civil history of the Jews that this event is of interest to the Christian, but as a part of the history of the inner life of us all. For, while the letter of the Holy Bible treats of outward and earthly things in the language of a parable, its spiritual or inner meaning everywhere relates to the religious experience of man and to the history of the soul.

Now, the first general maxim or moral which

we derive from this narrative is that which is so forcibly stated in its very words: "The Lord seeth not as man seeth; for man looketh on the outward appearance: the Lord looketh on the heart." This is a truth everywhere admitted and frequently urged in our relations one with another. We cannot too carefully bear it in mind when it comes to applying it to ourselves. We are all ready enough to urge it upon others for their adoption. Let us remember to apply it to our own conduct as rigidly when we are formimg our own judgments of those around us. "The Lord seeth not as man seeth; man looketh on the outward appearance: the Lord looketh on the heart."

It is true that we are not to blame for not being able to judge as God judges, for we cannot read the interior motives of another; we cannot look directly on the heart of another. This power belongs to Him who is All-seeing, who alone can look through outward appearance to the inward reality. For this state

of things we are not to blame; and all that
God requires of us is, that we remember that
what we see is only the appearance, and, remembering this, that we obey his command,
"judge not, that ye be not judged." And,
moreover, if we remember this, that God
alone, and not man, sees the heart, then we
shall know where to look for the only justi-
fication and approval of what we ourselves
are and do. Whatever men think and say of
us will be of less importance while we remember that they judge only of the appearance;
but it will be all the more important, yea, the
one all-important thing, that before Him "who
looketh on the heart" we can present a conscience void of offense. How many miseries
grow out of our forgetting and our misapply-
ing this Divine rule of judgment! On the
one hand we allow all kinds of ill will and
hatred to grow up between ourselves and our
neighbor, by judging that which we cannot see
and know,—his motives, his heart. Since we

cannot see his motive, we immediately con-
struct one for him to suit ourselves; we lend
him a motive out of our own evil will, and in
this way the judgment we form surely falls back
upon ourselves. We see things done that are
unjust, distasteful to us; wrong, as it seems,
beyond any question. We cannot regard.
such things as right, we cannot make them
seem right to us by any ever so friendly regard for him who did them. And it is not required of us that we should do so. Wrong
which seems wrong to us must remain wrong,
and be treated as wrong. But thus far we
may go and no farther. We dare not, cannot,
say that the same thing which seems wrong,
and is wrong to us, is equally wrong to him
who did it; because the motive of the deed is
what determines its quality of right or wrong,
and this motive lies in the heart, which God
only can see. The deed may truly be as
wrong for the doer as it is in our eyes; but
of this real guilt of the deed there is one

judge only, that is God, who alone sees the
heart, and who alone can judge the motive of
the deed. Another evil which we make to
ourselves out of this false mode of judging is,
that we allow ourselves to be influenced far
too much by what we think *will be* the judgment of men, and far too little by what we
feel *to be* the Divine judgment. There should
be no higher satisfaction, no more perfect
peace of mind, than the approval which our
own conscience gives to a deed done in the
fear of God. But how prone we are to think
that this will be a poor reward, to have God's
approval only, while all the world's opinion is
against us! And so we often choose to sacrifice all the blessed quiet and peace of a heart
pure in its intention, before the eyes of the
Most Holy, for the temporary approval of
those about us, who are so short-sighted as
that we can make fools of them by the false
part we are playing. I say by the false part
we play, for whenever we disobey our con-

science in order to please men then we play a
false part. For to please men we pretend
and appear to be and do what they love.
Now, if this be what our conscience tells us is
wrong, then we know that we are really doing
wrong to those whom we pretend to be loving
and serving. We know that we are doing
that which they are simple enough to believe
is out of pure love or integrity of heart, but
which we, on the contrary, know comes from
mere love for ourselves, the entire disregard
of their good, and the worst perversion of
reason, which is cunning. But there is also a
way of pleasing others and doing them kind
deeds which conscience approves, and this is
real charity, real honesty. For then that
which appears in our deeds, and which men
love us for, is the same as that which is in our
hearts, and which God sees and approves.
And this is to do to others as we would that
others should do to us ; this is to be perfect,
even as our Father in heaven is perfect.

Having learned this very needful lesson
from the literal narrative, let us look deeper
into its spiritual meaning, and see what particular experience or duty of the religious life
is here described under the figure of David
being chosen king.

Since all the personages here represent
things of the mind, the choice of a king evidently symbolizes the selection of some principle in the mind to which we will subject
ourselves, the elevation and consecration of
something in the heart to bear rule over all
our inward and outward life.

There is in each of us some affection, disposition, or some general motive which rules
over our whole life. Generally speaking, we
are all ruled over either by love to God and
the neighbor, or by the love of self and the
world; and under this general ruler there are
many subordinate rulers: such as the love we
have for our various pursuits in life; the love
of wealth or fame or applause, or of sensual

things; love of friends and kindred. All
these latter affections may be made to serve
and promote either the óne or the other general
or supreme love. But our hearts are not controlled directly by our love or affection for a
thing, but always by means of a certain power,
which we call the truth. This comprises all
things of thought and of the intellect. The
heart rules by means of our thoughts, our
reasonings, our conclusions. And when we
set up over our life any fixed rule of thinking, judging, reasoning, and planning, this
we call our *principle*, be it religious, moral, or
civil. We say a man is a man of principle
not because he has such and such affections or
motives, but because he has *chosen his king;*
he has established a certain fixed rule of judging and determining how to act. He has a
principle to refer to,—that is, some fixed stand-
ard of the truth as he regards it, by which to
judge of the right or wrong of things. Now,
the great true principle for a religious man is

the principle of the Divine Truth revealed in God's Word and taught in the Church. And a man subjects himself to this principle when he is a man of faith, when he is truly a believing Christian.

The very word *Principle* is almost the same as Prince, and means much the same thing. Therefore we can easily see how it is that the choice of David to be a prince or king over Israel is really, when spiritually understood, the same as the choice of the Truth to be our King, or the ruling Principle in the spiritual Israel, of our inner man.

In obeying the truth we are obeying God as our King, and because David represents the Divine Truth, therefore, frequently in the Scriptures, he represents the Lord; and when our Saviour comes into the world as the Truth or Word, it is with the declaration, "I am the Root and offspring of David, the bright and morning star."

An examination of our subject will give us

much light as to how men are to recognize or
know the Divine Truth, and how they are to
select the right and not the wrong kind of
principle to rule over their life's conduct. Let
the reader follow for a moment the events as
narrated. We find Samuel at the outset in
danger of making an improper choice, and just
so are we ourselves. For everything in our
present and our eternal life depends upon
what kind of a king we choose to govern our
thoughts and our acts. But this choice is left
wholly to ourselves to make when we come to
the age of discretion and see passing in re-
view before us the various candidates for
our adoption. How often is our mistake just
that which Samuel made when he saw Eliab,
Jesse's first son, pass before him! He looked
on his stature and his countenance, and, without inquiring further or seeking to learn anything of the heart, or actual quality of the man,
said, "Surely the Lord's anointed is before
me." Such is our judgment of the motives or

principles which present themselves to our
natural hearts for our adoption. We behold
the stature and the countenance, the outward
appearance, and if these be imposing and
pleasing, we exclaim readily, in our enthusiasm,
"Behold the anointed of the Lord." We look
for that which is imposing and conspicuous,
which will make a sensation and attract attention. We are pleased with that which is new;
we welcome the first-comer; we will do this or
that thing just because no one ever did it before us. Or else, to take a deeper view, we
are delighted at the intellectual grandeur of a
system of doctrine; the form and stature, the
outward appearance of the system of religious
belief we adopt is, we think, such as the world
will admire, and we admire ourselves in it; we
think, too, that because as a system of truth it
is so complete and entirely convincing to the
reason, that therefore it will, without doubt,
of itself make right the heart and the life.
We think that merely believing such a doc-

trine, merely recognizing such principles as
ours, merely choosing such a Prince, is the
very salvation itself of our souls. Whereas,
on the other hand, we have little taste for what
is old and commonplace, what others have
tried before us, what is neither noisy nor conspicuous, nor in any way calculated to reflect
any splendor upon ourselves. Deeper still,
we ask not ourselves what effect will this or
that principle of conduct, or this or that religious doctrine, have on my heart and thus on
my life, but rather what will men think of it,
and what will they think of my judgment and
my morality if I adopt it. In a word, in select-
ing a principle to rule over us, it may be the
Divine Truth, the Decalogue itself,—we are
inclined to make the most important consideration that of intellectual belief and outward
profession, and to forget almost wholly that
power which they are to have over the heart
and life for good, and which makes them
to be truly the anointed of the Lord. And

many there are in this day who, in their zeal
for a new and imposing Prince over the universe of mind, do not hesitate to ridicule the
old and venerated instrumentalities of faith, of
piety, and of religion,—of those things, in a
word, which engage the heart of man. They
declare that henceforth pure Reason or Positive
Science, or a perfect system of Social Econ-
omy,—some scheme at least of man's devising
which shall dispense with Divine Revelation
altogether,—that these are in the future to
take the place of religion and the Church.
How many a vain and pernicious system of
Philosophy and Morals is paraded in this cen-
tury, like a tall and handsome Eliab, before
the wondering eyes of a world craving the ex-
citement of some new thing! How many on
hearing of this or that new project for the enlightenment and advancement of the world,
caught by the glitter of some intellectual
sophistry which hides the corrupt and demor-
alizing spiritual tendency hidden beneath, are

ready to cry out, "Surely the Lord's anointed
is here!" Have we not seen one religious
sect after another spring up with its enthusi-
astic throng, gathering numbers rapidly for a
time, and crying out to all passers-by, "Behold, the Lord's anointed is here;" and
yet learning by sad experience that to regenerate a man, to make him from being
natural and self-loving to be spiritual and
truly charitable, something more is needed
than the adoption and profession of any system of faith and doctrine, be it ever so true
and ever so enlightened. " Man looketh on
the outward appearance : the Lord looketh on
the heart." And when Samuel so judged, lo!
all the seven sons passed by and yet none was
chosen.

And then did they send for that one, the
youngest, who was tending the sheep; for him
whose thoughts were not on ruling over men,
and making a fair appearance. And David
was brought in, and in the presence of his

brethren he was anointed the chosen of the
Lord.

David tending the sheep is the truth which
guards the innocent and holy affections of the
heart from corruption and violence.   To such
remains of holy truth stored up in the mind
by God's gracious providence must we all
come for that which He has anointed to rule
over and save us.   Whatever principle of conduct, whatever doctrine of faith, is present for
our adoption or our confidence, this must be
the main and only consideration which shall
determine our submission to it: does it guard,
preserve, and nourish those affections which
are innocent, which are of disinterested love
to our neighbors, and of reverence and sub-
missive love to the Lord?   It is only the shepherd-boy who can receive the Lord's anointing.

In choosing such for a king over us we shall
find this truth to be more and more the re-
cipient of the Divine goodness.   Our hearts
will by means of such truth become anointed

with the holy oil of the Divine love. From the obscure and retired place in the mind where, half ignored and forgotten, the holy precepts of faith still kept watch over some heaven-implanted affections of what is good and true, these same precepts are to be brought forth and elevated into their proper position of authority, and rule over all the thoughts, affections, and acts of our life. He who looketh on the heart will abundantly bless those who from the heart have chosen the Word of God to be their Ruler, and this not because they are convinced of its truth merely, nor because to believe it and profess it is the way of the world and what men approve, but rather because it and it alone can teach them how to cleanse their lives from sin, and how . to keep themselves unspotted from the world. Such is the meaning of David being called from the sheep-folds and the tending of flocks to be anointed in the midst of his brethren and made king over Israel.

XI.

The Armor-bearer made Harp-player; or, the Divine Truth protecting against Evil Spirits.

And it came to pass, when the evil spirit from God was upon Saul, that David took an harp, and played with his hand: so Saul was refreshed, and was well, and the evil spirit departed from him.—I. Sam. xvi. 23.

A SCENE in the court of ancient Israel, of that kingdom which was established in the world, and whose history is written in the pages of sacred Scripture, that it might be the representative of a kingdom which is not of this world,—the kingdom of the spiritual Israel, the kingdom of the Church of the Lord.

In this beautiful narrative of the troubled king sending for the young man, recently from the sheep-folds, to come and play the harp in his presence, so to bring quiet and rest to his

194

soul, we see depicted a hidden experience of many a Christian heart, which seldom finds its expression in words, except in that wonderful Book which alone reveals to the soul its own secrets.

David is comforting King Saul, playing the harp in his presence, and driving away the troublesome spirit of evil

Who and what are these persons, that the Word of God, given for the instruction and edification of our souls, should tell us so minutely about them?

All kings, representing as they do the governing wisdom and power, stand for the Truth, or the Law by which all things are to be ordered, and the stability and welfare of all maintained. The Lord, the one true and eternal King, because He is the Truth itself, and therefore the Law itself; by his wisdom He governs the world: and all power in heaven and earth belongs to Him also. Therefore all kings mentioned in the Scriptures are typical of the

Lord as to his Divine Truth.   And the Lord
is King and is called a King, and represented
by the kings mentioned in the Scriptures on
account of his being the Truth itself; for by
his Truth, which proceeds from and is the
form of his Goodness, the Lord rules the
world.   Therefore it is that to Pilate's question, Art thou a King, then? our Lord replied,
Thou sayest that I am a King.   To this end
was I born, and for this cause came I into
the world, that I should bear witness *unto the
truth*.

It is a turning-point in the history of Saul
and of David at which occurs the incident
before us.

It is as truly a picture of what afterwards
took place in the Humanity of our Lord, when
He as the Truth and as the King stooped to
earth and to our corrupt nature, and in Himself made that nature Divine by making the
Truth to reign in it, and so bringing it into
harmony with his infinite Divine Goodness.

Hitherto is Israel divided from Judah. Saul is king over Israel, but Judah is in the hands of the Philistines.

The king chosen of God, called from the sheep-folds, anointed by the prophet Samuel with the holy oil, to be the successor of Saul, to subdue the Philistines, and to unite the two kingdoms in one is the youthful David, the son of Jesse the Bethlehemite.

And because thus chosen and called away from the sheep-folds of Bethlehem to receive the holy anointed oil, to be king in place of Saul, and to unite Israel and Judah into one glorious kingdom, whose citadel should be at Jerusalem, whose Temple and King's house is Zion, therefore does David pre-eminently represent the Lord Jesus Christ, and his career is the great prophecy which in symbolic language describes the growth and the glory of the reign of the Messiah. Therefore is David so frequently mentioned in the Psalms and the Prophets when the great King of heaven—the Lord in his Divine Truth—is meant; therefore also is our Lord in the gospel called the son of David, and his spiritual kingdom called the kingdom of our father David. For, as remarked above, David, his calling and anointing, and his ruling over the united kingdoms, Israel and Judah, represents the Truth in the Divine Humanity of our Lord Jesus Christ.

When our Lord came to earth, He came as God to put on the nature of man, that He thus might come to men to rescue and redeem them. He could come to us only by becoming as we were; He could become as we were not by a change in his own Divine nature, for as God He cannot change, but by making our nature more like to Himself, and thus enabling us to draw nearer to Him. He came in his own Divine Unity and Perfectness as the one only Good and the only Truth. But by his Truth He entered into our flesh and nature, and so illumined it and purged it of evil that

then his Divine Good could also flow into it,
and thus humanity be restored once more to
that Divine Image in which it was created.
Because the Lord entered into our human
nature to drive out the devils that held it in
bondage, and to wash out its stains by means
of the Truth which is his own eternal Word
and Wisdom, therefore it is said that the *Word*
—that is, the Truth—was *made flesh*, and hence
our Lord is called the Incarnate Word. By
this is not meant that the Lord as to his
Love and Goodness, which is the Father, did
not also, as well as the Divine Word or Truth,
come to inhabit and glorify that humanity
which is the Son, but that first the Truth purified and rendered worthy the human nature
as its dwelling-place and tabernacle, and that
then came the Divine Good to dwell in it.
For when the Lord, as the Word or the Son,
had purified his human nature through his
victories over all the evils common to mankind and inherited from the Virgin Mary, then

the Father, which is the Divine Good, dwelt in Him and was one with Him.

First, then, was to be established the kingdom of Truth before, in the whole mind, love could reign. First must the truth, finding a foothold in the memory, the understanding, and the belief of a man, do its cleansing work in driving out the enemy, in discovering and overcoming the errors and the evils of life. Then comes the reign of love and goodness, when the regenerated will has the control, and the two kingdoms of the intellect and the heart—of the belief and the affections, of knowledge and of inclination—are no longer divided, but are united in one under the peaceful sway of "the Law that is written in the heart." This is the reign of David over Israel and Judah in the holy city Zion. It is the reign of the glorified Lord Jesus, in whom Goodness and Truth, the Father and Son, are forever united, and who is "the one King over all the earth, the one Lord, whose name is One."

Israel and Judah are the two kingdoms of the Holy Land, which under Saul were separated and at war, under David were united and at peace. They represent the two kingdoms in every mind, which by nature and inherited evil are divided, and which by regeneration of the Holy Spirit become more and more united and reconciled,—the kingdoms of the intellect and the will.

Saul lived in troublous times. He was king over the Israelites, but Judah was in the hands of the Philistines. He represents the Truth ruling in the intellect, in the beliefs and opinions of a man, while yet his heart is invaded by wicked affections. The Truth should not only be believed in the intellect, but it should be loved also in the will. But Saul, the king, was never to rule over the two kingdoms; and why?

Because Saul, when the Lord sent him out to battle with Agag, the heathen king, instead of destroying his enemy and his spoil, saved

ı*

the best part of the spoil and spared the
life of Agag. Therefore said the Lord's
prophet to Saul, "Thou hast rejected the
Word of the Lord, and the Lord hath rejected
thee from being king over Israel." Saul
saved the best part of the enemy's sheep and
oxen, instead of destroying all, as the Lord
had commanded. So does the man · who,
knowing the truths and the duties of religion,
uses them only partially in destroying the
enemy of his soul, condemning and regulating
only the lesser faults of his life, and still cher-
ishing to himself his greater and his dearer
evils. When the truth is thus false to its
stern, heaven-given mission, it becomes the
unworthy, the rejected king. It holds the
intellect in its power for awhile, but it
can never reform the will, wherein the real
evils of a man's life are rooted, because it
spares what the Lord commands it to utterly
root out and destroy. For a time the truth,
thus false to its work, thus putting on the

semblance of faith, but void of charity and the
real religion of life, may seem to be the principle of a man's belief and opinions; but at
length it is turned into cunning falsities, hy-
pocrisy, and craft. Like Saul, it not only fails
to unite the two kingdoms in one, but it loses
its power over its own. Truth without goodness, faith without charity, becomes the rejected
king. There must be a successor, who will
be the truth-believer from the love of goodness, or faith warmed and quickened with
charity of life. So Saul must yield the kingdom to David. And Saul, representing the
truth actuated and employed from selfish aims,
ceases now to represent the Lord; whereas
David, as the Truth ruling from the love of
Good, becomes the true representative of Him.
Therefore is the Lord called the Son, the
Heir of David; and the throne and kingdom
of David are frequently mentioned when the
spiritual and eternal kingdom of the Lord is
meant. Truth loved and believed, not simply

as intellectual stimulus, but as the law, the form, the moulding principle of the will and its affections,—such truth will battle manfully with the Philistines, will conquer the holy land of the affections from the hold of the wicked and idolatrous lusts, and will bring the heart and the mind, the affections and the beliefs, of a man into a harmonious subjection to the Divine Truth, as the Law of God's goodness, and will own as its King, the eternal Word, the very Messiah or Anointed One whom David typified,—Jesus Christ, the Lord.

Saul is the truth separated from the good of life, ruling for a time in the intellect of man. David, his successor, is the Truth believed in from love, obeyed in the will and its affections, and thus set up as king over the whole domain of the soul. David was called from the sheep-folds to be anointed king in place of the false, the hypocritical, the unworthy Saul. For so does the Truth, which shall save us, occupy itself in guarding the holy and innocent affections of good, represented by the sheep of Jesse the Bethlehemite; and out of the remains of heavenly affection implanted by the Lord in every soul during infancy and childhood comes forth the desire to believe, the willingness to learn, to understand, and to obey the law of truth which God reveals. Thus from some innocent affections of the will, enlivened by God's Holy Spirit, as by his call of the prophet, even while the heart is still held in the bonds of sin and death, comes that germ of faith, that young but mighty principle of heaven-born truth,—David the beautiful youth, the valiant warrior, the anointed king of both Israel and Judah. He is the faith which shall struggle with all the sins of self-love and spare none, and which rules finally in heavenly and peaceful sway over the undivided kingdom of the soul.

How often do men find themselves in the condition of the melancholy and troubled King Saul!—possessed of the mighty weapons

of truth, and all the valiant equipments of
reason, learning, and argument; well taught
in God's Word; knowing well their duty, and
knowing well their sins and the strength of
their foes; and yet, from faint-heartedness,
fearing to struggle with them; even in time of
temptation and actual combat, only half resisting, only half conquering; that is, thinking it
very wrong, but yielding nevertheless in act;
condemning the whole host as from hell, and
yet saving to themselves Agag the chief evil
of all, and the choicest of his sheep and oxen!
How should we not be troubled like King
Saul in such a time? And how could it be
otherwise than that the evil spirits will draw
near to us and torment us, entering into the
evil affections which we still secretly cherish,
and there striving for dominion in our heart
and making our conscience and our sense of
duty and our faith only troublesome and an-
noying to us? How often are our minds thus
divided and disturbed! and how often does the

Lord permit the evil spirits from hell to draw near and rouse this inward unrest, in order to teach us that true rest and peace is to be found not in a house divided against itself, but in the holy Zion, the kingdom of the good King and Lord, where not Israel alone, but Judah also, not the intellect only, but the heart as well, is obedient to the one Law of Truth and Goodness,—the rule and kingdom of Jesus Christ!

Well will it be for thee, reader, if in such states thou dost as did King Saul. For he made David to be his armor-bearer, and he called him before him. And when the evil spirit from God was upon Saul, David took an harp and played with his hand: so Saul was refreshed and was well, and the evil spirit departed from him. And so make David, the truth believed from the desire of goodness, thy armor-bearer; let thy knowledge and belief of true doctrine, which is the soul's armor and weapon, let this be animated and sup-

ported and carried into action by the desire to
be better, to conquer evils, to bring the whole
mind into subjection to God's kingdom; and
then, when thou art troubled in soul and
vexed by the presence and the insinuating
spell of evil spirits, call to thee this youthful
David, this harp-player, this heaven-anointed
truth of good, this fearless, this calm and
peace-bringing faith of charity. Pray to God
that the innocent and holy affections of good
may be revived in thee, that so all holy truth
and doctrine may be valiant in driving away
the evil counsel and the anxious forebodings
and doubts which invade thy peace. Recall
some wholesome truth of practical duty and
use, and strive, with the Lord's help, to per-
form it; and, if it be at first coldly, unwill-
ingly, still pray that the Lord make thee
willing; that He give thee the love of per-
forming it; that He send into thy heart the
heavenly delight of doing his holy law. And
this He will surely do. For his yoke is easy,

and his burden is light. And David, who was a valiant warrior and bore the armor of the king into battle, also knew how to play the harp so sweetly that the king's troubled soul was at peace and the evil spirit departed from him. So indeed shall every holy truth which we faithfully use in battling off and destroying the evils of our life come to us in our troubled moments freighted with heavenly comfort. It shall bring with it sometimes the harp, as well as the implements of war. The holy states of innocence, the good affections, the peaceful thoughts awakened in us by the truth thus present in our minds as the ruling principle of our lives, will be to us, sometimes, as a strain of unutterable music floating down from the depths of heaven, where the hand of Him whom David only typified strikes a harp of celestial harmonies.

18*

XII.

The Money in the Sack; or, How the Truth makes Free.

*And he said. Peace be to you, fear not : your God, and the God of your father, hath given you treasure in your sacks : I had your money. And he brought Simeon out unto them.—*Gen. xliii. 23.

THESE words occur in the story of Joseph. To understand something of their spiritual meaning it is necessary that we first see their connection with that interesting narrative. The leading facts of this story are easily recalled to mind : how that having been sold by his brethren and carried down into Egypt, Joseph was there after a time exalted by Pharaoh to be ruler over the whole land; how that he stored up corn in great abundance, so that when at length a famine prevailed the people of all the countries round about were obliged to come to him to buy corn; how at length

even his brethren, the sons of Israel, or
Jacob, came down also to buy corn, and how
they were treated kindly by Joseph, who knew
them but did not make himself known to them,
and how, on returning with their corn, they
found their money returned to them, each man
his money in his sack. Then they go down a
second time for more corn, and this time take
back with them their younger brother, Ben-
jamin, whom they had not taken before, and
whom Joseph had commanded them to bring.

And now arriving in Egypt, they are brought
to Joseph's house, and they begin to fear on
account of the money which they have found
in their sacks; for they think they have been
suspected of not having paid for their corn,
and that therefore they are now to be taken
captive and made bondmen to the ruler of
Egypt. So when they come to the door of
Joseph's house they say to the steward, "Indeed, sir, we came down the first time to buy
food: and it came to pass, when we came to

the inn, that we opened our sacks, and, behold, every man's money was in the mouth of his sack, our money in full weight: and we have brought it again in our hand. And other money have we brought down in our hands to buy food: we cannot tell who put our money in our sacks." And the steward answers them in these words : " Peace be to you, fear not: your God, the God of your father, hath given you treasure in your sacks : I had your money."

Now, this story describes in its spiritual meaning the experience of every religious man,—that is, of every man who believes in the truth which God has revealed, and is trying in some degree to obey it, and thus to reform his life. The truth itself,—that which makes up the substance of our faith,—this is what is described by the silver, or the money which the brethren of Joseph brought with them wherewith to buy corn ; and the corn of which they were in need represents the bread of the soul, that which sustains our spiritual life, namely, good affections, or the will to do that which the truth teaches.

The instruction we derive from this narrative, as spiritually viewed, is, then, something concerning the use we are to make of the truth. How is the truth we know going to procure for us that goodness of heart of which we are in need,—without which, indeed, the soul will die of famine? The answer is a brief one: we must give up bare truth, or the *knowledge* of what is right, in exchange for the desire and will of *doing* it, of acting it, of living by it. By giving up the truth, like so much money given in exchange for the corn, is not meant to abandon it or to depart from it, and to cease to believe in it, but it is meant to give it up as our own, to cease to believe in it, or to obey it as coming from man, and not from God. We give back the truth to Him who first gave it us; we bring back the money found in our sacks when we submit ourselves to the authority of the truth as to God's authority;

when we obey the truth, no longer because it is ours, but because it is God's.

This is what is meant by the sons of Jacob bringing back their money with them into Egypt when they came the second time to buy corn. And, therefore, it will be observed, their experience resembles that of any, at any time, who have tried to do this thing spiritually. They are brought to Joseph's house, and there they begin to be anxious and afraid, and to think that some great loss and misery is to befall them. They begin to fear lest, on account of that money which was found in their sacks, Joseph will seek occasion against them, and will fall upon them and take them for bondmen and their beasts with them. For when a man has been taught the truths of Christian doctrine,—that he must obey God, must keep the commandments, must examine himself and find out what are his besetting sins, and give himself no rest until he has resisted and conquered them; that he must act from

spiritual and not from natural motives ; that
he must be willing to suffer persecution and
worldly adversities rather than to disobey the
voice of his conscience, which is the holy Spirit
of God dwelling in him,—when a man, I say,
has been taught these things, and, moved by
the Divine Mercy and Grace, has begun to
think of putting them to practice and resolutely set his face toward heaven and the Lord,
in the desire to do that which is needful to save
his soul, what is his first experience in this
new casting about for spiritual life, for the
food of his immortal nature ? He knows that
life means something more than mere eating
and drinking and clothing the body, and that
at the best this corporeal and earthly life is
only a thing of a few years' duration. Christian doctrine tells him that his soul is to live
forever ; that after death there is eternal life ;
that beyond the grave there is an eternal
world ; that there is heaven and there is hell ;
that to one of these abodes the soul must go ;

and that he is himself responsible as to which
it shall be. He knows, too, that God holds
him to strict account for the deeds of this life,
—not in any caprice or merciless power, but
because of the laws of his own Divine Order,
and of man's existence, which require that
man, in order to live, must act in freedom, and
that as his acts are good or evil, pure or im-
pure, truthful or untruthful, such must his
whole nature become; and such as it has become in this world, such must it remain to
eternity.

Now, all these truths, when not only well
learned and remembered, but when grounded
a little in the heart and become really the belief
of a man's mind, begin then to exercise a kind of
compulsion over the outward life and the natural thoughts and inclinations, which compulsion is in nowise agreeable or welcome. These
stern and solemn truths of God's Word are a
little too much believed in to be hastily dis-
missed the mind; for they have led us on a

little way toward reforming our life, and so far
they have struck their roots down into the heart,
and begun to work a change in our inner affections, to form a new will within us. So, even
if we should determine in some evil moment
of temptation to cast off at one stroke all
these sacred and warning thoughts within us,
we find that even this is not so easily done!
In a word, the truth we know has sent us on
its mission; it has compelled us to go out and
procure some actual good, some real charity,
and purity of life. We are sent down to the
land of plenty to buy corn for our hungering
souls; *we are brought by compulsion to the
door of Joseph's house.* We are come into
that state of life when our external man is
ready to be united with the internal man;
when we are, in some degree, ready to let
the interior affections of truth and goodness
come down into and control the deeds of
our life in the world. And here at the very
door of this conjunction,—just here where the

question arises as to which is better, to let
the world and the body—the natural man, in a
word—have dominion, or the spiritual man
within, with its holy precepts of religion and
of eternal life,—here is where the first real
anxiety and difficulty arises. We think of the
money in our sack which is not ours, which
does not belong to us, and which is now perhaps only going to be the means of our losing
our own liberty and all that belongs to us.
We shrink back with a kind of dread from
that power and authority which we see that the
truth and religion must have over us, *if we
acknowledge it to be Divine!* We see that if
the truth is not ours, not the dictate of our
own will, but of a higher Will, to which ours
must be submitted, then we have nothing left
that we can call our own. This *internal, spiritual nature will have entire authority or none!*
Everything of selfish and of worldly love must
be given up. We have to deny ourselves,
to substitute for our human preference the

direction of God's revealed command, and to
have no wishes, no delights, no attachments,
no hopes of our own, but only wait for God to
send us that pure affection for what is true and
good, which the angels have.

This is the prospect of the religious life, which
will present itself at the outset of our efforts
after goodness, and which, at the door of
Joseph's house, will send anxiety and dread
into our hearts. "It is all," we say, "to be
laid to that silver which was given to us as
a free gift. Yea, all this comes of those
Divine, those holy truths which have sunk
down into our memories and hearts, and which
we cannot root out now if we would. There
they remain warning us, counseling us, direct-
ing us, bidding us seek the true way of life,
pointing unmistakably at our more secret evils,
and allowing no peace to our wounded consciences. If they were truths of our invent-
ing, things that we had constructed out of our
own fancies and imagination to as easily over-

turn again and forget; if it, indeed, were our own money, then it would be otherwise,—then, indeed, had we perhaps never set out on this search after the bread of life. But, as it is, the truth has not only shown us the way to satisfying our souls' need, but compels us by a kind of silent authority of its own to go seek this food, and even at the risk, as we at length discover, of our natural freedom and all that the selfish heart holds dear."

Thus does religion put on at the outset a certain dreary and dreaded aspect; such for a time seems the spiritual life when viewed from the position of mere natural affection and worldly wisdom. But this being the appearance only, how is it with the facts of the case? Do we really lose our freedom when we submit ourselves to the law of Divine truth? Do we really lose our happiness, the best things of heart and life, when we make our natural man subordinate to the spiritual? How was it with Joseph's brethren? Did Joseph, then, fall upon them and take them captive and treat them harshly? Far otherwise: he gave them corn and made them come in to the feast he had prepared for them, and made himself known to them as their own brother. And in reality we find in our experience that instead of losing our freedom and our happiness, the only way to preserve it is to obey the truth, not as our own but as God's, and to let the faith of the internal man be the ruler of our outward life.

For, even thus far, in obeying the truth, in doing whatever single act of repentance, have we not acted freely? I have said above that the will compels us; that it brings us to Joseph's door and there threatens to make us captive. We have perhaps been driven, in obeying the commandment, by fear of punishment hereafter, by fear of losing heaven, and this fear has thus in some degree compelled us. But, still, when it has come to a matter of acting in any particular crisis; when a temptation to do wrong has come in our way, and we have resolutely resisted and overcome it, where was the compulsion in that instance? Hard as the struggle was, have we not voluntarily chosen our part? Did it not lie before us to do this way or that, precisely as we of ourselves determined? This is certainly the experience of every one who has ever resisted temptation. No man in temptation feels himself to be a machine, a mere unthinking tool, to be handled by another's will and intention than his own. He *knows* that his own will and intention is what alone will determine his action. So I say a man acts freely in thus obeying the truth, in thus making the truth to be law over him. Our Lord says, "Ye shall know the truth, and the truth shall make you free."

And how as it regards happiness? Will our submission to God's law as over against the law of our selfish and sinful hearts render us happy? In the end it will, for this is the very kingdom of heaven which we all pray for. But even in this world where there is almost a constant combat between truth and error, where the evils of others are always adding to the misery caused by our own,—even in this world, I doubt if there be anything that gives the soul such a sweet, refreshing draught of pure happiness as the consciousness of having resisted an evil, having overcome a temptation by our own free, resolute choosing to obey the commandment of God.

And so it proves, in the result, that the life of religion is the freest life we can lead, and the happiest. We cannot but feel in every step we take forward in spiritual life that we have become just so much more free, and have been real gainers, not losers, of all that is worth possessing. We find the more we strive to obey God's truth as, Divine and not our own, just so much the more do we seem to act of ourselves, yea, as if it were our own ; for the truth seems to be ever more and more in accord with our own will,—not with our depraved, carnal, and selfish will; against this, indeed, ever clashing with this, and showing up its enormities, but ever more and more in accord with that new will which, by the grace of God, has been secretly and gradually forming in our inner man.

The freest beings in the universe are the highest angels of heaven, whose only will it is to do God's will; yet it is *their* will, *their* willingness, *their* desire to do God's will, and hence they do it in the fullest delight of heart. They do it feeling conscious that they *act from their own will*, not from compulsion, not as a lifeless machine. The truth of God is become their faith, it is their truth, because they have confirmed it in their life, and because they love it in their hearts; and yet they know it always to be God's truth, and as such they love to do it.

And it will be the experience of every man, that the more he attains to real goodness of life the more he will seem to act freely as of himself, untrammeled by any outward influences or circumstances. And this is illustrated by what we further read in our story, that Joseph's brethren said, "We have come again to buy food, and other money we have brought wherewith to buy it." That is, they do not ask now the corn in return for that money which they found returned to them in their sacks, but for that other money which is their own. And the steward seeing that they both acknowledge the money given them, and at the same time are willing to pay other money which is their own for their food, bids them fear not, for God had given them their money in their sacks, and, moreover, their money had come to him. He recognizes their willingness to pay for their food, and at the same time tells them that God has restored to them the same that they gave. And this is the whole lesson: that if *we will give up our natural freedom to God, He will give us back spiritual freedom, and with this, natural freedom, too.* If we obey the Di-

K*

vine truth in opposition to our sinful will, God
will enable us to obey it afterwards willingly,
as our own and because we love it and take
delight in doing it. In a word, the whole story
goes to confirm that great doctrine of the
Church, that we must *Shun evil, because it is of
the devil and from the devil; and we must do good
because it is of God and from God; and that in
thus doing the truth we must act freely of our
own choice and from our own hearts; but at the
same time acknowledging and believing that all
our will, understanding, and power to do this is
in us and through us from the Lord alone.*

THE END.